MISSION:
Merry Christmas

Nancy Naigle

MISSION: Merry Christmas
Copyright © 2020 Nancy Naigle
All rights reserved.
Print ISBN: 978-1-948320-06-1

Publication Date, September 2022

Crossroads Publishing House
P.O. Box 144
Patrick Springs, VA 24133

Dear Reader,

After eight full-length Christmas novels, I hope this little sweet snack of a book will be easy to fit into your busy schedule, and help you keep things in perspective during the annual holiday scramble.

This is part of a series of "shorts" that I've written with the busiest readers in mind. Something with enough story to touch your heart, but short enough to get through when time is tight, or you just need a quick pick-me-up.

I hope the fun and sunshine in MISSION: Merry Christmas will give you the energy to complete all your holiday to-dos on time with a smile.

Wishing you a Christmas that's the merriest of all, with a touch of that laid back island relaxation, so you can enjoy every single moment the magic of this holiday and your family traditions brings to the season all wrapped up in a pretty red bow.

Merry Christmas,

Nancy

NOVELS BY NANCY NAIGLE

Adams Grove Series
Sweet Tea and Secrets
Out of Focus
Wedding Cake and Big Mistakes
Pecan Pie and Deadly Lies
Mint Juleps and Justice
Barbecue and Bad News

Boot Creek Novels
Life After Perfect ♦ Every Yesterday ♦ Until Tomorrow

Antler Creek Novels
Christmas Angels ♦ What Remains True

Seasoned Southern Sleuths (aka The Granny Series)
In For A Penny (Free in Digital Format)
Collard Greens & Catfishing ♦ Deviled Eggs & Deception ♦
Fried Pickles & A Funeral ♦ Wedding Mints & Witnesses ♦
Christmas Cookies & A Confession ♦ Sweet Tea and Second
Chances

Stand Alone Novels
Sand Dollar Cove (as seen on Hallmark)
The Secret Ingredient (as seen on Hallmark)
Christmas Joy (as seen on Hallmark)
Hope at Christmas (as seen on Hallmark)
Dear Santa (Mass Market – The Christmas Shop)
Christmas in Evergreen I, II, III (as seen on Hallmark)
A Heartfelt Christmas Promise
Recipe for Romance
The Shell Collector (as seen on FOX Nation)
The Wedding Ranch
And Then There Was You
…and more.

For news from Nancy about sales, new releases, and movie
updates, sign up for her newsletter or download a printable
book list at www.NancyNaigle.com.

ACKNOWLEDGMENTS

Sincere thanks to my friends and readers who helped bring charm to this story by way of suggestions on the characters careers, setting, and how to bring a snowy white Christmas to a child for the first time in a place where Mother Nature doesn't share that beauty.

Luckily, the magic of the season teases the imagination just enough to make everything seem brighter and more memorable at Christmas.

CHAPTER ONE

Avery Troupe's gut had been spinning since the moment she'd received email notification of the meeting with her boss at four o'clock this afternoon. First of all, Tom Ware never worked in the office on Mondays this time of year when New York City turned cold and grey. Second, late afternoon meetings had a long history of being bad news around here, and Tom wasn't great to be around, even on a good day.

As the day drug on, and she hadn't heard anything else from Tom, she dreaded the meeting even more.

Just before four, Avery sucked in an extra breath for confidence as she approached Tom's door and leaned in the doorway. "You wanted to see me?"

Tom flashed that smile he was known for and leaned back casually in the oversized executive chair. "Avery. Yes, come on in."

Her nerves settled cautiously. "Is everything okay?" Hundreds of colorful twinkle lights on the

Christmas tree in the corner of his office cast an almost Santa-like glow over Tom, distracting her for a moment.

Tom was the furthest thing from a jolly old soul. No matter what seemingly kind of act he was up to, he always has an ulterior motive.

She'd learned that the hard way when she'd first started working at The Ware Agency. She'd quickly learned that his ego was even more inflated one-on-one than the highly dramatic personality that dazzled the obscenely high-paid sports figures he represented. She loved her job, but Tom was Tom, and like now, everything had to be a production.

His eyes darted to the shiny ornaments on the Christmas tree. "Every shiny ball on that tree represents an athlete represented by The Ware Agency."

"I know," she said sarcastically affirming him. Each ornament hung like a trophy. Nothing Christmassy about it. Bragging rights is all it was, and if it was one thing Tom was good at, it was bragging. But he was her boss, so she smiled through it. "It's been a great year for the agency."

"Yes." He nodded. "Yes, it has. My most profitable year yet."

He slid an envelope across his desk.

"What's this?" She picked up the envelope. It wasn't standard Ware Agency letterhead. Turning the fancy holiday envelope in her hand, someone had taken the time to write her name in beautiful calligraphy across the front.

He tapped his fingers together slowly in front

of him. *More Grinch-like than Santa.*

"Open it." He nodded toward the envelope. "I think you'll be pleased."

She *had* gotten that hockey player healed in time for the playoffs, which sealed the Stanley Cup for them. That had earned another fancy feather in Tom's cap. Maybe it was another bonus.

Anticipation motivated Avery to remove the contents. It was a check, and the five zeros following the number made her nearly stagger. This was over-the-top, even for Tom Ware.

"This is *very* generous." She sat. *Clearly, I made the nice list.* Her smile pulled so wide her lips quivered. "I'm... wow. Thank you."

"See how much value I put on your hard work and the wellness program you manage? I recognize the changes you've put in place have been a factor in our significant growth this year."

Pride flooded over her. It was true, but hearing it from him was a big deal.

Her whole heart and soul were poured into that wellness program. She'd built it, staffed it, and managed every aspect of it. Starting out as a sports therapist, it hadn't taken long to realize she had much more to offer.

Pitching Tom Ware about building a preventative and maintenance plan for all their athletes, not just the injured ones, to keep their moneymakers healthy had been scary, but thankfully he'd jumped on the opportunity.

The wellness program had proven to be a win-win. It had also been the differentiator that had

3

landed them some of the biggest names in the business this year.

"It's worked out well for everyone," he said.

It always came down to the money for Tom, but she took pride in what she'd built here. She'd found a way to make a real difference. This was more validation than she'd ever dreamed of.

A pang of guilt stabbed Avery's gut for thinking of Tom as the Grinch.

Tom leaned forward, his forearms resting on the fine leather insert on the desk. His smile faded. "Look, I appreciate all you've done…"

Something in the way he hesitated sucked the joy out of the room. Dread washed over her.

"Our new business model now separates us from the competition with the wellness program as a key part. We've set the bar. The others can't touch me now."

The unspoken "but" still dangled like a glass ornament too close to the edge of the branch.

"The players have responded well," Avery said. "They've been really committed to the plans I've put together for them. I'm proud of what we've been able to achieve in such a short time. The data shows a significant reduction in injuries already over last year." She shifted the check to the other hand, its invisible strings tethering her excitement.

"I agree," Tom said. "But I'm afraid I'm going to have to let you go."

The check crinkled in her hand. "What? You can't—"

"I can. That's a generous severance." His thick

finger hung in the air, pointing at her.

"I built that wellness program from the ground up. Our clients are counting on me. You can't just fire me."

"Technically, I'm actually eliminating your position."

She shrank back as each stinging word landed. "Eliminating?" She hadn't expected this. Torn by conflicting emotions—confusion, anger, disbelief, and pity on him for thinking he could replace her so easily. Her mind spun, leaving her without a better response.

"I can. I just did, and technically, that wellness program and everything else you worked on under my employment belong to me. The legal team has confirmed that. You're under contract to The Ware Agency, and that makes all of this intellectual property mine." He pushed a document toward her. "It's all here. You remember signing this non-compete, don't you?"

She did. She'd have signed anything for the opportunity to build the wellness center. It had been her dream come true. "How can you do this? We're friends." In the polite way. Not *real* friends. "It's almost Christmas."

"So do a little shopping. Start celebrating early."

Her mouth dropped open, but no words came out.

"You'll land on your feet," he said. "You're that type. Just don't mess with any of my clients. It's in your contract. Of course, you know better."

"I know better?" Her anger flared, but at this point, she wasn't sure it even mattered.

"I'd hate to ruin our friendship with a lawsuit," Tom said. "Take the check and turn your back on all the clients in my portfolio. I'll make sure they get everything they need. No sloppy goodbyes. No contact at all. Understood?"

She couldn't absorb anything he'd said after the point of *your position was eliminated.* Something more had to be driving this. He'd just handed her a huge amount of money. "This doesn't make sense. I don't understand where this is coming from."

He stirred uneasily in his chair. "Violet and I are getting married on Christmas Eve in the Hamptons."

"What does that have to do with me?"

"She's not comfortable with our...past."

She laughed. "We don't have a past. What did you tell her?" Sure, they'd been to Paris for the Tour de France, the polo championships in Palermo, and the Super Bowl together. Even New Year's in Times Square with clients, but none of that had been personal.

"Does it matter?" He shrugged, that smile turning more smug by the second. "The point is, removing you will make Violet happy, and frankly, I've already hired a replacement for about a third of what I'm paying you. Everything is running so smoothly; I doubt anyone will even notice you're gone. We'll just replicate the plans you've put in place for the new clients."

"You can't do that. Those programs are

designed for the individual needs of the athletes. It's not a one-size-fits-all." She should let him just fumble the whole program, but her good intentions wouldn't allow her to let it go.

"Not yours to worry about anymore." He leaned back in his chair again.

She couldn't help but wish, for one teensy second, he might topple over. "This is the thanks I get for helping you grow your business? When you hired me, you were just another sports agent struggling for the next big thing. Now, star athletes are coming to *us*." She had to keep herself from wadding up that check and throwing it right at his smirking grin.

He checked his phone. Wishing she'd disappear, no doubt. "That check is thanks enough," he said flatly.

She wondered how ironclad her contract was. Most non-competes weren't worth much more than the paper they were printed on. She'd built a reputation in the sports world now. Surely, he couldn't stop her from taking on clients if they contacted her directly. Or could he?

"Don't cause a scene, Avery," Tom said. "This is the way it has to be. Look at it this way. Now you have plenty of time and money to Christmas shop. Enjoy."

The money was nice, but being out of work wasn't how she'd planned to spend the holidays. She sighed. Tom was only in it for Tom. This shouldn't surprise her.

"Merry Christmas." She pasted a smile on her face, then turned and walked toward the door.

Don't be bitter. Just hold your chin up and walk out, she coached herself.

"Avery?"

She stopped but didn't give him the satisfaction of turning back around.

"I'll need the keys to the corporate apartment by next Friday."

That part hadn't even entered her mind yet. It just keeps getting better. No job and *no home for Christmas.* She closed her eyes, hoping she wasn't going to cry. She blew out a breath and faced him.

"Of course you do. How about I send the keys with the wedding gift?" She closed the door behind her and walked straight out of the building. There wasn't anything in her office she couldn't live without. All she wanted right now was to get as far away from The Ware Agency as she could.

CHAPTER TWO

Even after reciting the chain of events to her sister over the phone, Avery still found it hard to believe she was out of a job.

"He fired you?" Corinne's disbelief echoed in her head.

"I wasn't fired." Avery scowled. She hated it when Corinne's voice went up that way. Avery wanted to be consoled, not judged. "Fired is what happens to someone when a person doesn't perform. I performed. Exceeded all expectations. I took his business to the next level. I raised the bar for the whole industry."

"Call it whatever you want. It sounds like he fired you."

"Eliminated my position," Avery mumbled.

"You're out of a job either way. What a jerk. I told you that dating in the workplace was a bad idea."

"Seriously? We're going there? I didn't deserve this. We didn't date. I wasn't anything more than an arm piece for him in public to a few

9

games, and that was like two years ago. History."

Okay, so they'd been major sporting events and very public, but they weren't romantic or cozy. It had been her job. Fun at the time, but boy, did she regret it now.

"Well, apparently it looked like more to someone, because it's biting you in the butt now, isn't it?"

"You mean Violet?" She'd spat the name, which wasn't fair. Violet was very capable and deserving of her position at the agency. It was hard to believe she'd agreed to marry Tom, but then that was Violet's problem, not Avery's.

"Yeah. Maybe Tom, too. Who knows? I guess all that matters now is that your life is going to change, and you have the opportunity to move in whatever direction you like. It could be a good thing."

Corinne had always been the bright-side-of-the-picture girl. It drove Avery nuts.

"Doesn't feel very good," Avery muttered. "I hired Violet. You'd think she might have been grateful for that." The blood pounded in her temples.

"I'm sorry this is happening to you right here at Christmas," Corinne said. "He couldn't have waited until the New Year?"

"On the bright side, the severance pretty well covers Christmas, New Year's, and practically to Memorial Day."

"That was generous," said Corinne in her ever practical way. "So, what are you going to do?"

"I have to be out of the apartment in a week.

I'll find somewhere to stay and then figure out legally what I can do for work since I signed a non-compete with him."

"Don't worry about that. You're good at what you do. It'll sort itself out. You know you can always work for me. You're over-qualified for most of the work, but it'll pay the bills."

Corinne ran a huge network of traveling nurses and health-care professionals. Before Avery decided to specialize in sports medicine, she had worked for Corinne.

"I've got some money put away and this big check. I'll be fine once I find a place to live."

"We have plenty of room. You can stay as long as it takes you to figure out where you're going to land."

"Thanks, Corinne. The apartment was furnished, so it's really just my clothes and a few things. I could put everything in storage, I guess." Going back home to Vermont for the winter and spending some time with Corinne would be nice. It had been too long between visits, with work being so busy.

"Just ship all your stuff here." Excitement grew in Corinne's voice. "We've got room in the garage. I know it's lousy circumstances, but I can't wait to see you. How many years has it been since we were all together for Christmas dinner? Mom and Dad will be so thrilled. But we have to do it at their place. Dad still isn't getting around that well."

Avery's muscles froze. "Wait. Corinne. I can't." She sucked in a breath. "They'll know something's wrong."

"Oh, yeah. You never did have a good poker face."

"Dad will freak out if he thinks I'm out of a job, no matter how much money I've socked away. We can't put that stress on him right now. Not so soon after the last episode."

"You're right. He'd give himself another heart attack," Corinne said.

"Once I figure out my game plan, I'll go see them, but for now, it's better if we keep this quiet. In fact, I better not stay at your place. The kids would blab for sure."

"Mom and Dad are going to know something's up when they don't get the standard issue outrageous Ware Agency fruit and gift basket."

There wasn't anything standard issue about those oversized baskets. It was embarrassing, really. Avery snorted. They were so tacky. Tom had a team of five full-time employees putting those baskets together. It took them almost three months to assemble, then three weeks to hand deliver them via limo to every client. Tom insisted on sending them to the leadership team families as a perk. Last year, there'd been gift cards and freebies from the brands represented by his athletes, like underwear, tennis shoes, liquor, jewelry, and even breakfast cereal. It was a weird combo, but not surprising that Tom would want to flaunt his reach. He thrived on throwing his accomplishments around like confetti in a one-man parade.

Avery knew exactly how she could fix that.

"I'll make one and send it with a fake card with the agency logo on it. They'll never know the difference."

Corinne's sigh taunted her. It wasn't fair to ask her to keep the secret. "Please don't tell them," Avery pleaded. "Not until I figure out what I'm going to do. Please?"

"Actually..." Corinne stretched the word out about two syllables longer than it needed to be. "This might be perfect timing, *and* the answer to your problems. For a little while anyway."

"You have that tone in your voice, like the time you tricked me into sinking my sausage patty into Dad's coffee."

Corinne's laugh made Avery laugh, too.

"Dad still doesn't believe you put me up to it, even after all these years."

"Excuse me while I straighten my halo," Corinne teased. "I promise it's not anything like that, but it would really help me out. A favor for a favor?"

"You're making me very nervous. Like the next words out of your mouth are going to be, 'Your mission, should you choose to accept it...'"

Corinne giggled, but didn't deny it either. "I have a client who has been a bit of a challenge."

Avery could tell that was an understatement, just by her sister's tone.

"He's fired the last four people I've sent down there," Corinne explained. "I wasn't going to send anyone else, but now his sister has stepped in. She's asked me to send a sports therapist, not just an aid. You've handled these kinds of patients a thousand times over. He won't give you any problem at all, and you can't beat the location."

"Where is it?"

"In the Caribbean islands. Palm trees. Sunshine. Powdery beaches. The bluest waters you'll ever see. The only downside is Mr. Cranky."

"I can handle Mr. Cranky. What's the injury?"

"Mountain bike incident. Knee, and according to the doctor, it's healed. I think it's more about getting the patient to do the therapy so he can keep the injury on the down-low with the team. Should be a cakewalk for you."

"Routine." Even the worst patient couldn't ruin a free trip to the islands during the winter. "Sign me up."

"Done. You really are saving me on this. It's nearly impossible to get anyone to work over Christmas. When can you leave?"

Avery looked around her apartment. "I'll grab some boxes and ship my stuff to your house, then pack. Won't take too long. I could be there Thursday."

"That'll work. I'll send you the flight information and the rehab reports. His sister sent me everything."

"Terrific. I'll work up a plan before I get there. Thanks, Corinne."

"You can thank me when you come back with a tan and spend New Year's Eve with us. Dan talked me into hosting the party this year. You have to come. Deal?"

Avery wouldn't miss that for the world. "Count on it."

CHAPTER THREE

Icy rain washed over New York City as Avery boarded the plane for paradise, and Corinne had sweetened the deal by booking her in first class. Avery tucked her damp jacket in the overhead, then grabbed a blanket and settled in for the flight. She pulled her feet up in the chair and worked on her Christmas shopping list. It was cut by more than half now that there'd be no obligatory office gifts to shop for.

Truth was, she could probably make the list in her head at this point. It was so short.

It would definitely be a bigger challenge to put together that enormous fake Ware Agency gift basket while out of the country, but she'd figure something out. Or maybe she wouldn't.

Wasn't it bad enough she hadn't told her parents her position had been eliminated? Perpetuating the lie only made it worse. She'd have to tell them after the holidays, anyway. Why not let Tom Ware look like a forgetful, uncaring jerk? It would only prove her point.

She crossed the fake gift basket off the list.

The flight was surprisingly smooth once they got out of New York. She daydreamed about warmer weather as she stared out the window into the puffy clouds. It looked like she could walk across the sky from here.

Finally, the pilot announced their initial approach. They'd be landing soon, and she hadn't even thought to crack open her novel.

Avery took in the beauty below. White sandy beaches and royal blue water that twinkled in the sunlight. No one here had a clue she had no job, no address, and no idea what she'd do with herself next year. But for now, it was island time, and she intended to keep reminding herself of that to ward off those fearful feelings of frustration.

She stepped out of the airplane into balmy temperatures, thankful she'd dressed in layers. The warm air resuscitated her. Like an animal coming out of hibernation, she took in her first deep breath since she'd deposited that severance check. *This too shall pass.* She rolled back the cuffs of her long-sleeved blouse as she made her way through customs. A few quick questions later, she grabbed her bag off the carousel and headed for the cab line.

Rich music from a steel drum band outside the airport lifted her spirits, and suddenly the bright colors made her wish she'd worn something a little more fun. It took her a minute to realize the calypso sound was Jingle Bells. The full-out "Dashing Through the Snow" version. No one around here would be dashing through anything but sand on this island, but even so, they were in the holiday spirit.

She straightened her black blouse over her slacks. A bright pink and lime green taxi pulled to the curb. Not sedans like in the city. This thing wasn't much bigger than a Mini Cooper, but somehow the driver wedged her bag into the back.

A stack of different colored pine tree air fresheners hung from the rear-view mirror, giving off an odd, but not unpleasant, cherry-vanilla-leather scent. She plucked at her top, hoping for relief from the air conditioning, which unfortunately wasn't blowing nearly as much as it was making noise.

She sat back as the car pulled away from the curb and navigated the route to the far side of Horseshoe Cay. There were only a few cars on the road. For the most part, people cruised around in fancy tricked-out golf carts and motorized bikes. Her driver whipped by them as if they were traffic cones.

The houses at this end of the island were much nicer than the small cottages near the airport. In fact, some looked more like resorts than homes.

Maybe they were.

Don't get your hopes up. With her luck lately, she wouldn't be surprised if the on-site amenities for this assignment weren't much more than a hammock on the beach. Although, in this weather, even that would be fine.

Just get through the holidays and follow the tide into the new year.

They finally slowed to a stop in front of tall, scrolling gates.

"This is the address," the driver said in an elegant island brogue—almost melodic. A nice change from the brusk northern accents back in the city.

"All right, then. Let them know Avery Troupe is here. They should be expecting me."

A high-pitched buzz squelched when he pressed the intercom, but no one responded. They sat there, waiting patiently as the heat rushed inside. He pushed the button again.

She checked the paperwork her sister had given her. There wasn't anything about a gate on it, and definitely no code.

"Are you sure it's the right address?" He looked hesitant to try again.

"14772 Coopers Cay."

"Yes. That's what's written here on the monitor."

She dialed the phone number. "Let me call." More of a grumble than a greeting came over the line. "Good afternoon. This is Avery Troupe. I'm here to assist Drew Martin."

"You're here already?"

She shrugged toward the driver, who appeared slightly amused.

"Yes. We're at the gate." The buzzer sounded again, and then the gates opened. "Thank you."

In the short time the window was down, the thick air had evacuated the air conditioning, and now her hair clung to her neck.

The narrow driveway twisted between hedgerows of some kind of tropical plant with thick branches and large, glossy leaves. She could just imagine the number of snakes and lizards slithering around, comfortably camouflaged in the thick shrubbery with other critters that loved the heat. Probably spiders as big as her hand. She shuddered, trying to knock that image from her mind. There'd be no jogging down this path while she was here.

The driver glanced in the rear-view mirror. Was he wondering how far this road went too?

The landscape changed from jungle scrub to clean and sleek as the house came into view. Vibrant tropical flowers swayed in baskets hanging from hooks along the porch. The place had an almost southern plantation feel to it. Very *Gone with The Wind*, except it had wraparound porches on both levels, and instead of white, it was painted a buttery yellow. Navy blue stairs to the front door picked up the same color as the shutters.

The driver parked in the circle drive near the porch. She took out her phone and sent the pin drop to her sister with a short text that read:

Avery: Had no idea this place was going to be so nice!

Corinne: Hot-shot athletes. Go figure.

Avery tucked her phone into her purse and got out of the car. The driver had already deposited her bags on the front porch. She thanked him and walked toward the door as he sped off.

CHAPTER FOUR

Drew heard the doorbell ring but didn't budge. He'd left the front door unlocked just to see how long it would take this one to let herself in out of the heat.

The little voice in his head told him not to leave her standing there, but the other voice, the one that tempted him to prank his teammates, urged him to see for himself. *Just a little test.*

He turned the volume up on the television and sat there with a smirk.

The doorbell rang again, twice this time.

If only he'd had the forethought to not answer the gate when they'd buzzed earlier, he could've pretended he wasn't even home.

"Hello? It's Avery Troupe."

He heard the roll of suitcase wheels along the natural stone tile, click-clacking along the grout lines.

"Excuse me?" She flipped the light switches, the whole room illuminating at once. She left her bag and walked over to where he sat in front of the television, half-watching Sports Center.

"I let myself in when you didn't answer, Mr. Martin."

"Mart—? Oh, yeah." He muted the television. Avery Troupe was not what he'd expected at all. Pretty for sure, but not like the women who had traipsed through here as assistants the past couple of weeks. Those had seemed more like candidates for the next casting call for The Bachelor than actual help. None of them seemed to have been qualified for much more than sunning by the pool and ordering takeout.

Avery's gaze held his, and she didn't look ready to give in.

Her auburn hair hung past her shoulders, the ends curling this way and that, making him want to reach out and smooth them. Drew's twin sister Brooke always complained the humidity messed up her hair like that, too, but he liked the curls.

Drew gathered himself. He hadn't intended to be anything near impressed, but she seemed not only willing, but capable, and well, frankly, pleasant.

"Thank you for coming," he said. "I had a misunderstanding with the last person they sent."

The lift of her eyebrow told him she'd probably already heard about it. Now he could tell his side of that story.

"I didn't ask for help. My sister set this up. I'm focused on training, so what I need mostly from you is to just keep things out of my way. You know, go through the mail. Field phone calls."

"Oh, really?" She took in a long slow breath, her

smile spreading in a way that made her look even prettier. Unlike the other woman who had shown up dressed to the nines, Avery Troupe stood before him, all five-foot-seven-ish of her and in obvious good shape, wearing a nice pair of black slacks, a sports top with a blouse over it, and sneakers. Actually, she looked ready to work.

"You see, Mr. Martin," Avery said, "I'm here to get you through rehab. From what I understand, you injured your right knee. Nothing too serious, but you're off your game. After looking at the physician notes your sister provided, you are not meeting the physical therapy goals that he'd set."

"I'm doing the physical therapy."

She folded her arms across her chest, crossing one leg over the other. Her legs looked very long. He tried not to stare, but failed.

"Doing the prescribed exercises on your own?" she asked.

Drew bristled. Who did she think she was? "Yes. I'm quite able to get through an exercise program."

"Well, let me get settled in, then I'll walk you through what I'm being paid to do, and how I will guarantee you that, with my help, you will be where your doctor expected you to be a few weeks ago before the end of the year."

Drew laughed. Well, she'd already proven to be more capable than the last one. That girl had stood out there sweating for over an hour. By the time he went to see if she'd given up and left, he'd found her sitting on the front porch fanning herself with one of the fallen palm fronds. "Yeah. That's fine.

The cleaning service just left. Your room is at the end of that hall. Make yourself at home."

"Excellent," she said. Her mouth opened, but then she seemed to stop herself. Without a word she pasted a smile on her face and gave him a quick nod. "Great. I'll go get unpacked, and then we can discuss your rehabilitation plan."

"Okay," he said.

When she turned away, he saw that her shirt was soaked where the sweat had dripped down her back in the very short time she'd waited outside. The temperatures were unseasonably warm even for here this week. He regretted leaving her out there like that, now.

She dragged her suitcase down the hall.

He turned up the television and kicked his feet up. He hadn't done his exercises yet today, and had missed a few here and there, but he just hadn't felt all that well.

It wasn't ten minutes later when he heard her coming back into the living room. Her shoes were doing that squeaky number on the stone tile. He hated that sound.

Before he could turn to greet her, she was standing right between him and the television screen.

He leaned to the left.

She did, too.

"Okay. Yes?" Pretty or not, he wasn't sure he appreciated her tenacity.

"I thought you'd be ready to get started."

He looked down at himself then back at her and

shrugged. "For our talk about your plan?"

"Let's walk through some of it. You know, move your body."

"Oh." Reluctantly he turned off the television.

Her eyes went right to the beer bottle sitting on the end table next to him. "Is that from this morning?"

He looked at it. He honestly wasn't entirely sure if it had been or not. "Maybe," he said, locking eyes with her. Did she think she could just judge his lifestyle? What was wrong with a beer now and then?

"Have you had breakfast?"

He shifted his eyes toward the beer again.

"I didn't think so," she said. "Please tell me there are groceries in the house."

"There's no more beer." The joke didn't land as well as he'd have liked.

"Good. That's not on the list, anyway. We're going to have to set some rules about your nutrition."

He smirked, flashing his best smile. "Aren't rules made to be broken?"

"Not on my watch. Which way to the kitchen?"

She wasn't being nasty about it, just kind of take-control and matter-of-fact. She reminded him a lot of his sister. Brooke would love Avery.

He heard Avery go down the hall, and then cabinets opening and closing. The next thing he heard was the blender whirring at high speed.

She strode back into the room looking pleased with herself and handed him a tall Yeti cup with a bright red straw. "Here we go." She took a sip of hers, encouraging him to do the same. "This will get us through the morning, then we need groceries. Do you have a car?"

"A golf cart."

"Good. When we're done here, we'll go to the market."

"Bum knee." He pointed to the soft cast. "It's electric. You can drive it."

"If you want a say in the menu, I think you should drive. You're capable. Looks like you could use some fresh air, anyway."

He hunched down in his chair, balancing the glass on the arm of his recliner.

"Drink up. You'll feel better," she insisted.

He took a swig, then sputtered. "What the—" He sputtered, then stuck his tongue out and lurched forward, gagging.

Could he be more melodramatic? "It's not that bad," she said.

"It's bad."

"Maybe so after a beer. Your body needs the right nutrition to heal, build, and recover."

"Are you going to make me drink these every day?"

"I'm here for three weeks. That's fast, even for me. Once we go shopping, we can take that smoothie off the menu."

"Fine. I'll drive," he muttered, resolute.

"I thought you might see it my way."

"Are you always this sure of yourself?" he asked.

Her expression softened, her warm brown eyes

twinkling with a hint of fun in there somewhere. "This is what I do. So, yeah."

"You think you'll have me walking without a hitch in just three weeks?"

"If it's important to you, and you're going to take this seriously."

There was one thing he was serious about. Baseball. "I have to start training by January 1, or I won't be ready by spring." It came out more like a dare than a statement.

"If you do what I say, there's no way we can fail."

He stared at her wondering if all this bravado was for real. If she'd been a dude, he'd be high-fiving her right now, but this—from the likes of her—threw him off.

She pressed. "Do you want to play again or not?"

"Baseball is my whole life." He chugged his smoothie and put the cup down on the table. "We better get to the store. We've got work to do." He snagged his dark sunglasses and a ball cap from the counter then strode the best he could outside, with her at his heels.

CHAPTER FIVE

Drew had never spent that much time in a grocery store before, and they'd walked up and down so many aisles that his knee ached. He popped a couple ibuprofen and gutted through it though. He had to. People knew him around here. He couldn't risk anyone seeing him injured and word getting out.

Avery bought so many things that he worried they wouldn't be able to fit it all in the golf cart. But thankfully, he was a master at packing, and he'd been able to stack, tuck, and balance everything to get it home. There would be no more smoothies on the menu for at least the next week.

She waved goodbye to the men who'd helped her with the fresh fish and meat. She'd demanded good protein and lots of it. She'd come on big and bad with him right out of the gate, but she was friendly, and everyone they'd come in contact with had fallen right into her charms.

"What is that smell?" She shut her eyes, inhaling as he sped down the main road.

"That's elder. Those yellow flowers," he said pointing them out. Her eyes were still closed though, so he nudged her with his elbow. "Over there."

"They're so pretty! Stop."

He laughed and kept on rolling.

"Please. Stop."

He mashed his foot on the brake, and she jumped out and ran to the side of the street. She bent over and sniffed one of the yellow bell-shaped flowers. "This is my new favorite flower. Will I get in trouble if I pick one?"

"Probably." He motioned for her to get back in the cart. "I have a whole backyard of yellow elder. You can fill your room with them if you want. Swim in the bathtub with a pile of petals if it makes you happy."

"I'm very easy to make happy," she said.

He wondered if that was true. He'd been with a lot of woman, and he hadn't yet met one that he'd consider low-maintenance or worth the hassle. If he ever discovered one, he'd never let her slip away.

She climbed back into the golf cart, lifting her chin to the sky. "The sun feels so good."

"It's pretty nice," he had to admit as he adjusted his sunglasses and put his foot on the gas.

He drove up to the gate at his property, punched in the code, and then sped to the front door.

She reached up and grabbed the frame, but she didn't complain.

Drew unloaded the last of the groceries from the golf cart to the porch so Avery could take them inside, then parked the cart.

Just as he lowered the garage door, his phone rang. Finally, his sister returned his call. "What have you done this time, Brooke? You've gone from one extreme to the other."

"I take it help has arrived."

"You know exactly who has arrived. You're supposed to be traveling for work. Don't you have something to do besides getting up in my business?"

"You aren't taking care of it. You don't leave me much choice." Brooke's words cut when she was right.

He poked his head out of the garage. The front door closed. His words came out part snarl through clenched teeth. "You sent a sports therapist? She's in the business. She'll know who I am."

"Calm down. I gave you my last name."

"If word gets out, I'll never forgive you."

"Stop it, Drew. She came very highly recommended. She's not going to give away your secret. There are laws against that, and I'm sure she has her own reputation to worry about. I can't sit by and let you sulk after that last report from the doctor. Especially with me not in town. I'm so sorry I'm not there."

"How's it going?" He'd much rather talk about her than himself.

"Good. But you need me."

She was right. He did need her. Like most twins, the two of them talked every day, and although he was irritated with her, he wasn't mad. Never could be. "I'm fine, but thanks for saying that."

"Have you seen Nico today?" she asked.

She'd never had children of her own, but Nico,

her stepson, couldn't possibly be loved any more if she'd had him herself. He felt the same way about the kid.

"No. Haven't seen him since you left. Did you warn him to steer clear?"

"I might have. Doesn't mean he listens to me. Like you, that boy has a mind of his own."

He loved his sister, but Brooke liked being in charge, and that was fine as long as she wasn't bossing him around. He'd set himself up for this, though. When he took that tumble off his mountain bike in Colorado, he had played it off with the guys, but he knew he'd hurt himself.

He knew better than to mess around like that. It was even in his contract. If he screwed up this season, he'd likely ruin his whole baseball career. So, he'd hopped a plane to the only place where he was safe from the public eye: the small island of Horseshoe Cay down near the Exuma Islands where Brooke and her husband ran one of the finest resorts in the Caribbean.

"Nico's probably reworking his list to Santa," she teased.

"Don't remind me. I hate I ruined our plans."

"Stop. All that's important is we'll be together. It doesn't matter where."

"Easy for you to say. You're not eight. I'd feel better if you went ahead and took him skiing."

"It wouldn't be the same without you, and you know it."

He did. They'd never spent a holiday apart. After Drew had signed his last contract, he'd bought a house here as an investment, leasing it to celebrity visitors to offset the cost of owning a place here so he could visit whenever he wanted. Thank goodness, with Brooke's help, he'd convinced the people that were booked for the holidays to move over to the all-inclusive resort without so much as a hiccup.

So far, he'd kept the injury quiet. Not even his manager knew, but it made him nervous that this Avery woman was now in the picture. The sports world was small, and word got around fast. Especially when it was bad news.

"What's she like?" Brooke asked.

"She's barking orders like a drill sergeant already."

"Maybe that's what you need."

"She made me drive to the grocery store."

"Well, good for her. That's more than I've been able to get you to do. I feel good about this."

"Glad you do. I'll either be a hundred percent or dead at the end of these three weeks."

"Well, use this time wisely, because if you don't mend soon, it's not going to matter who kept your injury a secret, because there won't be any hiding it."

Brooke was only older by two-and-a-half minutes, but she'd always been the more responsible one. Everything she did was planned and calculated.

"Promise me you'll let her do her job, Drew. She's supposed to be the best in the business. Consider it your Christmas gift to me."

"I'd rather buy you a Ferrari and forget about it."

She laughed. "Wouldn't want one."

32

"Yeah. You're crazy like that. Quit sending me help I didn't ask for, and we'll be fine."

"Be nice to this one. You're ruining my good name."

"You shouldn't have booked me under your last name then. Drew Martin? Really? You couldn't think of something more original." Drew Laskin just hoped the pseudonym worked. Between the fake last name, six weeks of facial scruff, and foregoing a haircut, he was happy Avery Troupe hadn't recognized him at first glance. If he had the energy, he'd Google her to see just how good her reputation was.

Brooke laughed. "You can thank me now."

"Thank you." But as usual, he couldn't hold his tongue, if for no other reason than to give her a hard time. "I guess."

"I'll be checking in, and I'm sending Nico over to check on you tomorrow to make sure you're still alive."

Nico was wise beyond his years. He was a good kid, too. Better than Drew had ever been. Growing up on a resort probably made him more mature, and he and Nico had become quick buddies. Only now that Drew was injured, there wouldn't be any biking or playing ball. What the heck do you do with an energetic boy when you can only hobble around?

"Tell Nico to bring me chocolate," Drew said. "She didn't let me buy any junk food or beer. It's not going to be fun."

"Promise you'll behave?" Brooke asked.

"I promise." He jabbed the button to end the call. *Promises. Women always want promises.*

He shoved the phone in his pocket and limped back up to the house. He could hear Avery in the kitchen, probably still putting groceries away. Hopefully not making something horrible for him to drink.

He sat in his recliner and turned the television on.

"All right, then. I see you're in your favorite spot." Avery entered the room in a flurry of energy. She clapped her hands twice. "Let's get moving. I'm scheduled to be here exactly three weeks, and based on your file, I don't see any reason why I can't have you in ship-shape in that time."

"What? Now? We just got back."

"Come on." Clipboard in hand, she put her foot on the end of the recliner and pressed, sending him to an upright position.

Who the heck did she think she was? "Excuse me. I'm watching this."

She lifted the remote and turned down the volume. "There's only so much sports news. Trust me, I know it'll replay four times on four different shows all day long. We've got work to do, and I'm the one to get you where you need to be."

He sat there dumbfounded. *Be nice.* His sister's words tick-tocked in his brain. She was pretty, but her overly confidant, militant style could get old fast. Maybe he should have left well enough alone with the aides they'd sent. All they had really wanted to do was lounge by the pool and tan. At least they hadn't tried to tell him what to do.

"What makes you think you're so qualified that you can get me back on my feet and ready for spring training by the new year? Because in case no one has told you, that's what we're looking at here."

"Fair enough," she said. "I'll spell it out for you."

Why did I even ask? He was pretty sure he wasn't ready to hear the answer.

CHAPTER SIX

Drew watched Avery drag out her laptop, and open the D. Martin folder she'd already setup. She flipped through pie charts and bar graphs showing all the data she had put together for his rehabilitation schedule, while she explained her recommendations.

Her battle plan would make any Army general proud. Somewhere between his failing glutes, weakened thighs, loss of flexibility, and needing to improve his side-to-side asymmetry, he'd quit listening.

"English?" he asked as politely as he could, but the sarcasm hung in the air.

"You're compensating for the injury rather than strengthening the muscles that will help you heal. We can't just focus on the knee. The ankle, knee, thighs, hips, even those glutes—they all have to work together."

It painfully made sense.

"Look. I've been doing all these measurements so we can monitor your progress daily. I'll build long-term plans customized to you to reduce the probability of re-injury, which is even more important than the initial rehabilitation."

"I've been doing all the exercises they gave me. I don't need a physical therapist, and I have a perfectly good gym right here."

"Well, according to these reports, you're not making the expected progress, and lucky for you, I'm a sports therapist. I have a degree in sports medicine and my job isn't just to restore mobility. It's getting you back to optimum levels of functional, occupational, and sports-specific fitness." She slapped the cover closed on her laptop. "So, are you ready to do this, or not?" Her hair bounced behind her shoulder with the head nod.

He snorted. He hadn't meant for his reaction to be heard, but he'd been through hurricanes on this island that had less bluster.

Avery rose to her feet. "Now you look. I'm getting paid whether you improve or not. I'm good at what I do. One of the best. I've got references. I've helped professional athletes make strides doctors didn't even think were possible. I'm at your disposal. Let me help, or I'll just read a book. It's your dime."

They stared at one another for a long moment. If he had to guess, she'd stand there all day if that's what it took. He wasn't sure why he was fighting her except he was tired and aggravated. Aggravated that one slip of his foot was putting his whole career at risk, and that they'd had to cancel the family ski trip because of it.

He'd promised to teach his nephew, Nico, how

to ski and build a snowman. It would've been Nico's first white Christmas. How did you make that up to a kid? There were only fourteen shopping days left, and Drew still hadn't figured how to compensate for the giant let down.

He sucked in a long breath. "Fine," he said. "Ms. Avery Troupe, or doctor, or whatever it is I'm supposed to call you. You have a deal, but I'm not kidding around when I say absolutely no one can know about this. Not about you being here. Not about this plan. I will not give you a reference, no matter what miracle we pull off. Do you understand?"

"Completely. I'm bound by HIPPA. This is how I make my living, I'm not about to compromise my reputation for gossip. Believe me, we have the same goal."

"Well, then, I'm all yours."

He watched something pass over her expression at his unintended double entendre.

She cleared her throat before she spoke. "Great. You can call me Avery." Like a switch had been flipped, an enthusiastic smile spread across her face. How had he not noticed the sparkle in her brilliant blue eyes before now?

Wearing black yoga pants and a stretchy shirt that hugged every toned curve of her body, she carried an interesting aura of beauty and ability that intrigued him. He wasn't entirely sure if that was good or bad at this point.

She extended her hand. Something light and flowery teased his nose.

He stood and accepted the handshake,

embarrassed for the first time in weeks for the
disarray in the place. "Excuse the mess."

Her eyes held his, a wrinkle pulling in her
forehead. She nodded toward the huge fern tipped
over in the middle of the room. "Traffic accident?"

She didn't need to know he'd thrown it in
aggravation after he'd fired the last woman. "It
looks like it'll live, don't you think? I've never been
that good with plants."

Avery walked over and righted the palm, then
lifted the heavy pot and plunked it in the corner. "I
don't know. Looks like it needs life support to me.
How long has it been sitting there?"

"A while."

"Okay, well you're the priority. So, let's get
some measurements." She turned on the lamp, but
dissatisfaction etched her face. She marched across
the room and swept back the heavy curtains.
"That's better."

"Whoa." He squinted. "Just whoa. Whoa. Whoa.
Whoa-whoa."

"What's wrong, Batman? You allergic to light?"

Did she seriously just call me Batman? His eyes
watered as they adjusted to the bright mid-day sun.
All he could see was her silhouette against the wall
of glass windows overlooking the pool and outdoor
kitchen.

"Oh. My. Gosh. Seriously?" Her hands settled on
her hips. "You're sitting here in the dark with this
view? We're right on the water? And a pool? Why
didn't you mention that?" She nodded. "Oh yeah,
we're moving this workout outside. Come on. Hop
to it."

He had a feeling his pity party was about to end, and he wasn't even mad about it. He liked her spunk. She was right. It was a million-dollar view. Literally.

He was so sore from all the shopping he grabbed the crutches lying on the floor next to his chair and stood, steadying himself on them to lessen the pressure.

"You never saw this," he said to her.

He half-walked—more like a skipping hop—out to the patio. He took in the view as if she might when seeing it for the very first time. It wasn't a bad place to live. He'd better pull it together if he wanted to be able to afford to continue to do so.

CHAPTER SEVEN

Avery had Drew go over all the exercises he'd been doing on his own.

She shrugged. "Okay, it's a typical plan for the strain you've put on those ligaments, but no wonder you're not improving. First thing we'll do before any workout is warm up." Avery took Drew through the proper lower body stretches and added a few others to warmup his whole body, not just the injured part.

"This is taking longer than the exercises."

She put gentle pressure on his leg, helping with the stretch. "Do you have anything better to do?"

"No. I guess not."

He'd muttered the words like a teenager on restriction. "Just trust me," she said intentionally trying to be more caring about his situation. "Okay?"

He didn't complain anymore. He kept up with her and gave it one hundred percent. Maybe more, because he appeared to be completely tuckered out by the time they completed the warmup.

"That's it," she said.

His body wobbled like a wet noodle. "Thank goodness."

"Go change into your bathing suit. Now, it's time to start the real work." She'd be lying if she didn't admit that she loved the look on his face when he realized they hadn't even really gotten started.

Wearing her red tankini, she waded in the shallow end until he came outside shirtless. She felt the hitch in her breath at the musculature of his chest and shoulders. He was as tan as a man should be in the summer, in the middle of December. He looked good. Very good, except for that slight limp.

He dove into the deep end and swam over to her. His strokes were long and smooth, gliding through the water with ease. He stood, flipping his head, sending water everywhere as if he were a giant sheepdog on a rainy day.

She had to concentrate on the work, not him, no matter how good he looked. She didn't date clients, and she never, ever dated athletes. She'd had her one-and-done disaster experience with an athlete, and the rest of the world could ogle his blue eyes and slim hips all they wanted because that man would never settle down. He was married to the game, and she was never going to be anyone's second love.

An hour of pool work went by quickly. She counted out the exercises, slowing him down and helping him get the proper form. The poor guy was waning, but she had to give it to him for not giving up.

"Okay. Good job." She climbed out of the water and wrapped a towel around her waist. "You need to go through all of those stretches again tonight before bed. Let's get you inside and ice the knee. I'll make dinner."

"You don't have to cook for me." He walked to the side of the pool.

"I know that, but I've got to eat, too, and I'm not up for delivery pizza. Which, from the stack of empty boxes that were on your kitchen counter, seems to be all you've eaten for the last month."

"That may be regrettably close to the truth. I did order mushrooms, onions, and peppers on them though."

"That's not going to get your vegetables in."

"You don't count pepperoni as protein either, do you?"

"No. Here's the deal." He stood below her in the shallow end of the pool, and she leveled a stare at him. Suddenly, she felt like the mother of a teenager. "You can eat all the pizza you want…on New Year's Day. I'll even place the order myself before I walk out that door."

"I should order them." He reached for the railing and climbed out of the pool. "You probably don't have the experience to order a decent pizza."

He stood there, dripping wet, tan and well-muscled. She'd seen her share of awesome athletic bodies, but this one struck her. Maybe it was the set of his jaw, or that his body didn't match the straggly beard or the beer diet. Whatever it was, it left her a little off-balance. She shook off the thought, fighting to recover her strong stance on the subject.

"And you, my friend, need decent nutrition if we're going to make the progress I expect."

He walked toward her, not bothering to wrap a towel around himself. "Okay, okay. I'm all in." He crossed the patio. "I never had a trainer cook for me before."

"I don't usually do this type of assignment anymore. I'm doing this as a favor to my sister," she said as she picked up a towel and turned to follow him. "You don't know her, but believe me, we don't want to let her down."

"I have that kind of sister, too." He left wet footprints all the way to the door, but then stopped and faced her. She caught a quick breath as he stood there face-to-face with her, hands on his hips. She kept her eyes on his face, but the water droplets hitting the bricks were a distraction.

"So, we're going to do this? Right?" Goodness, was she talking about the rehab or something else? He looked good enough to—

Stop it!

She shoved the extra towel into his stomach to give herself some space.

"Right. Yeah. Looks that way."

"Good." She handed him the crutches. "You can use these if you need them. You've worked hard. Just remember they are called crutches for a reason. Don't use them any more than necessary."

"Got it." Rather than put the crutches beneath his arms, he raised them above his head and walked to the door under his own power.

She watched his gait. She'd seen worse. If he cooperated, he'd be happy with his progress by

Christmas.

Inside, Drew dried and changed into sweatpants before coming back out to the living room. She'd already changed and was waiting for him.

"Let me give that leg a good massage." She tapped the back of the recliner. "You can sit here. I've got a massage table being sent over tomorrow."

Drew didn't argue, taking a seat and pulling his pant leg up.

Avery massaged his leg with long smooth strokes. She closed her eyes, imagining the position and tenderness of the muscles and tendons beneath his skin. He didn't complain, although she knew some of it was less than comfortable. There were some things you just couldn't do for yourself in this type of recovery. "Sit tight, I'm going to ice you down." She left the room and came back with a gel pad that she wrapped around his knee and then secured it in place with plastic wrap. "How's that feel?"

"You're good at that. Good. I like what you did with the plastic wrap there."

"Tricks of the trade," she teased. "If nothing else I can teach you a few shortcuts."

"Every little tip helps. Thanks."

Their gaze held, then Avery looked away and got to her feet. "I'm going to go shower and change, then I'll get dinner going."

Fifteen minutes later, she was chopping and dicing fresh veggies. She'd never claimed to be the next top chef, but she knew her way around an air fryer, which she used to cook the fish they'd bought straight off the dock. The guy at the market had fileted them right in front of her.

She began plating the meal, pleased with how it had turned out. It had everything that his healing nutrient-starved body needed. In the pantry, she found a pretty poinsettia table runner, so she spread that across the dining room table, then set the table for two.

Drew came into the dining room just as she carried the plates in.

"I can take those," he offered.

She handed him the plates and followed.

She saw him notice the holiday table runner, but he didn't say a word before sitting down and placing his napkin in his lap. "This looks good. I could smell it all the way in the other room."

"You should be starving after that workout."

"I am." He set his hand on the table. "Glad you approve. Actually, it felt good."

"I'm sorry I came on so strong." She picked up her fork, but noticed he had his head bowed, silently praying. She hadn't expected that.

A moment later, he lifted his head and began eating. "You really think you can have me in good shape before the new year?"

"I do." The fish was cooked perfectly. It flaked as she put her fork in it. "You're not the first rookie to have an off-season mishap like this. Believe me, it happens. Life happens. You're going to be fine. No one will be the wiser."

There was that smirk again, followed by the snort. She had to tell him at some point just how rude and annoying that was.

"For the record, I wasn't being reckless. It was a

simple mountain biking accident. I was getting off my bike when I stepped on a loose rock. I would never do anything to risk my career. I love baseball."

He had that baseball player look to him. Tall with long legs, nice arms, and hair long enough in the back that it probably curled just right below his baseball cap. In her experience, most of them were pretty average, but this guy... he was good looking, and in really good overall shape. "What's got you so bent out of shape? I mean, look at you. You're a mess. Your sister is worried. It's got to be more than the knee. Or are you really always this way?" She hadn't meant that to come out so judgy. To lighten the moment she added, "That plant in the living room happens to agree with me."

He busied himself with the meal. Then he lowered his fork and swept a hand through his long thick hair. A lock fell forward.

Women paid big bucks for waves like that. Too bad he was an athlete, and technically a client for a few weeks. Totally off limits. Besides, she had way more important things to worry about right now than some hot guy with a luxury villa in the Caribbean.

Drew propped his elbows on the table. "There *is* more. You're right. It's not just about me. I've let everyone down." He looked up at the ceiling and then looked directly at her. "That doesn't make me happy. And no, I'm not usually this big of a jerk, but lately, I'll be honest, I just can't seem to shake this bad mood."

She regretted coming down on him so hard now.

"You said you weren't being reckless. It was an accident. Just move forward. Accidents happen. People understand that."

"It's not that simple. I'd promised my nephew I'd teach him how to ski for Christmas." He dropped his hands and stared at his knee. "There won't be any skiing this year."

"No. There won't be. I'm good, but I'm no magician. Seriously though, that's not the end of the world."

"It was going to be his first white Christmas."

"Okay. Yeah, that's bigger, but there will be others. Right now, let's get you well, and more importantly, help you find that good mood you said you have somewhere."

"Am I that cranky?"

"Yes."

"Is that supposed to help me feel better?"

She set her fork down, and glanced over at him, then away. "I guess I'm a little cranky, too." She looked back at him. "Please accept my apology. I'm usually much more professional than this." She let out a breath. "I'm here to work. I'm sorry we got off on the wrong foot. I've had a bad couple of days myself. Why don't we go back and restart this arrangement?" She stretched out her right arm. "Hi, I'm Avery. I'm here to help you speed up your recovery from this injury."

He laughed, taking her hand. "Drew. Nice to meet you. I could use a hand. No pun intended."

She laughed too. He wasn't as bad as he'd seemed at first. And after all, he was her mission. Getting this off her sister's plate was way easier than shopping for a present for her, or having to deal with her parents about losing her job at the holidays.

Avery gave him a nod. "The good news is that you didn't tear anything. You're behind, but I'll get you where you need to be. We can move into therapy without too much worry. We'll work hard, but careful. I have a feeling your nephew… what's his name?"

"Nico."

"I bet Nico will be happy to have his fun uncle around for Christmas, even if it means no skiing. Maybe you two could build a sandman instead, or we could make him part of the rehab. He'd probably have fun in the pool. Don't all kids love to swim?"

"I know you're joking, but he starts holiday break next week. Maybe we *could* do that. My sister is traveling. He'd love to hang out here a few hours each day. Would you mind?"

"Not at all. No one ever said this couldn't be enjoyable. I mean, look. You live in paradise. Just because you're injured doesn't mean you have to be holed up in your house."

His brow arched.

"Okay, I may not have made it seem like it could be fun, but you were lying around in the dark being Mr. Cranky when I arrived. I had to snap you out of it."

"I can't wait to see what fun looks like to you." He chuckled and shook his head.

"Hey! I can be fun," she insisted.

"That remains to be seen." He forked up another bite. "After that nasty shake this morning, I was afraid of what you might feed me, but this dinner is really good. Thank you."

"You're welcome." They ate in silence, and a more comfortable vibe fell over the two of them.

She got up to clear the dishes. "I'll bring the plates in the kitchen if you'll load the dishwasher. Then we can stretch and call it a night."

Once they finished cleaning up, she bagged up the trash. "I saw the trash can out front. Why don't you hit the gym for those stretches, and I'll take this out then catch up to you?"

"Whatever you say."

He headed to the gym, and she walked out the front door, then stopped. The sky looked like a canvas. Undeniably beautiful. The clouds stretched like great wings of pink and orange against a purple sky with the sun barely hanging over the horizon.

Blessings. Yes, maybe there was a silver lining to the bad hand she'd been dealt. This, for one, was a view she'd never forget. Beautiful and quiet compared to the noise of the city. Almost too quiet. The fresh air left her a little dizzy in a good way.

In that moment, the sun fell below the horizon.

She walked out to the end of the house and lifted the lid on the trash can, then screamed.

CHAPTER EIGHT

Drew put his hands against the wall. His quads stretched, loosening from the earlier activities. He held the position until he heard a blood-curdling scream coming from outside.

Moving as quickly as he could, hopping on one foot, he made it to the front door almost slamming right into Avery as she came high tailing it up the porch toward him.

He grabbed her forearms to keep her from crashing backwards. "What happened?"

Her fingernails pierced his forearms. On tiptoe she stuttered out an explanation. "It—there—oh my—"

"Are you okay?" he asked.

She pulled her hands back and leaned forward, trying to catch her breath. "I'm sorry. Yes." The words came out like puffs. "Snake? Lizard? I'm not sure." She leapt behind him. "In the trash can!"

He glanced over. The hinged lid was down. "Seems like a good place for him to stay to me."

"Scared the heck out of me. How did he get in

there?"

She seemed so tough a few hours ago. Fearless even. He was excited to see, at least she was human.

"They won't bother you," he said, trying to reassure her while at the same time stifling the laugh he knew would not be welcome at the moment. "I guess I should warn you that sometimes a few feral goats hop over the fence and trim back the flowers too. They won't harm you, either."

"You find this humorous, don't you?"

"Sort of. Yeah."

"At least you're healthy enough to rescue me now," Avery said. "That's further along than you were this morning when you claimed you couldn't drive the golf cart." She swept past him, then stopped in the doorway and turned back to him. "Don't you have some stretching you're supposed to be doing?"

"Right. Yes." He turned to face her. "I was in the middle of that when you went all damsel-in-distress on me."

"Pardon me?" She looked offended, but then her whole demeanor changed. "I wasn't *that* distressed."

"Could've fooled me. I heard you screaming from inside the house, down the hall, with the door closed, I might add. It sounded distressed." It was getting increasingly more difficult not to laugh.

She lifted her thumb and forefinger at about an inch apart, then widened the span. "A little distressed?"

Her half-smile told him all he needed to know. The next couple of weeks were going to be a lot more fun and interesting than he'd initially thought.

"Did you forget to start with the steam room before stretching?"

"Is that your polite way of telling me I need you to keep me on task?"

"Apparently so. In the morning, first steam room. Stretch. Then, we'll meet by the pool at eight."

"Yes, ma'am." He lifted his hand in a salute. "I'm on it."

Avery left him standing there, looking forward to the rest of this assignment.

Thank goodness he hadn't gone looking for the reptile, because her scream was surely more frightening than that little blue and green lizard. Avery just hadn't expected to see him staring at her, making that icky bloody-looking bubble under his neck, when she'd lifted the trash can lid. *Next time he can take out the trash.*

All in all, barring the lizard, it had been a good day. They'd gotten past the awkward stuff, the push-back, and had had a productive workout. He'd actually made it through a lot more exercises than she'd expected him to.

She changed into pajamas and laid across the bed, flipping through the channels for something to watch. Christmas was just around the corner, but it felt like summer here. It didn't help that Drew didn't have one single decoration in the house. The poinsettia table runner had been a lucky find, but even that was pretty subtle.

There wasn't much on television. She settled on a reality show between neighbors seeing who could out-decorate each other with Christmas lights. She texted Corinne to let her know things were on track. It took her no time to fall asleep after the hectic first day on the job.

The next morning Avery's phone rang in the middle of her yoga workout. She answered it on speaker, and continued the stretch.

"Hey, Avery. So, it's going smoothly?"

"It was a rocky start, but yes." Avery stood, and sat on the edge of her bed. "We have a plan. He seems committed to it."

"I knew you could do it. I owe you big time."

"Actually, I owe you. This place is amazing, and this job is keeping my mind off my problems." She glanced at her watch. She was supposed to meet Drew at eight, and it was nearly that now.

"We're not talking about those problems. Remember?"

"Right." She leaned back against the pillows. "Poor guy. He was worried to death. It was a rookie mistake, but he'll be fine."

"You didn't call him a rookie, did you?"

"I probably did. Why?"

"You really don't recognize him?"

The play in Corinne's voice came off as a

challenge. "Drew?" She crisscrossed her legs. "No. Well, he has a familiar look to him, but no, I definitely don't know the name or him. Should I?"

"He was only Rookie of the Year two years ago."

Avery couldn't place Drew Martin. Rookie of the Year? "Wait a minute." He was taller than she'd ever realized, but there was something in the rumble of his voice, and those dark eyes. Only usually, he was squeaky clean cut. And in all those commercials. How had she missed it? "Oh my gosh. I was so preoccupied with his attitude. It's Drew La—"

"Laskin," Corinne finished with her. "Sorry. His sister swore me to secrecy. I guess you can see why now."

"I can, but I can't believe you didn't tell me. That explains the blue and yellow colors on this house, too. Team colors. I thought it was a little odd. I mean, all the other houses on this island are pastels and beachy colors."

"Martin is his sister's last name. She and her husband live there on the island, too, but she's had to come to the states on business for a few days. I'm sure you'll meet her soon enough."

A tingle of dread went down her spine. "Corinne, we really might have a problem here."

"Why? If anyone can get him back on the field, it's you. You're the best at what you do."

"I have a non-compete. Remember? If Tom thinks I'm down here trying to woo Drew Laskin, there's no telling what he'll do."

"I didn't know he was a client."

"He's not, but he's on the top five list. Everyone has been working like crazy to get him moved over to us. Like, money's no object attack mode."

"If he's not signed with The Ware Agency, I doubt there's anything Tom could say about it, and frankly, who cares if he gets mad."

"I hear you, but really, I don't want to rattle his cage right before I know where I stand. I need to get my contract over to an attorney this week."

"He'll never find out," Corinne said. "Drew needs this to stay quiet, and you do, too. Seems like a perfect situation if you ask me."

She sucked in a breath. It *was* a nice place to hunker down for the holidays. "I have to tell him the situation."

"Fine. Tell him, but please don't blow it out of proportion. Tom will be so busy worrying about getting married, the last thing on his mind will be you."

The doorbell rang. "I've got to go. Someone is at the door, and Drew's in the steam room. I'll talk to you later."

CHAPTER NINE

Still in her yoga pants and tank top, Avery jogged from her bedroom to the door. Through the glass panel, she saw a bright blue golf cart parked in the middle of the driveway. And there stood a little boy.

She opened the door. "Good morning."

"Hi. I'm Nico." His dark black hair shone in the morning sun, making it look nearly blue. "Is my uncle around?"

"He is. Come on in." The young boy zipped under her arm and right by her, making a beeline for the living room.

Drew walked out of the steam room at the other end of the hall wearing a robe. "Hey, buddy. I didn't hear you come in."

"Mom said I could come over today."

"Yeah. That's great." They high-fived. "Did you meet my friend?"

Nico lifted his chin. "She let me in."

"Avery. This is my nephew, Nico." He leaned close to Nico's ear. "She's in better shape than the two of us put together."

The little boy looked impressed.

"She's helping me get ready for next season, and when we were talking last night, we were thinking maybe you could do some workouts with me in the pool."

"Maybe even some water basketball or volleyball, which I'm pretty good at," Avery bragged.

Drew shrugged and nudged his nephew. "Game on, right?"

"Yeah!" Nico had the biggest brown eyes she'd ever seen. He'd be a heartbreaker one day. Especially with someone like Drew Laskin as an uncle, who was known to be one of the most eligible bachelors in the league. She could still kick herself for not recognizing him.

"I have to do some stretches and stuff, or she'll write me up."

Avery opened the curtains. "Nico, you can help me get breakfast ready if you'd like."

"I'm good at helping in the kitchen."

Drew slapped the wall as he headed into the gym. "See you two in a bit."

"Take your time. Slow, long stretches, like I showed you last night," Avery reminded him.

"I'm a fast learner."

"Mom says Uncle Drew never listens."

"Does she now?" Avery gave Drew a knowing look. "I had barely noticed. We'll trust him to do it right. Let's go get breakfast ready."

Nico followed her into the kitchen. "Can you can get the fresh fruit and yogurt out of the fridge, please?" She gathered the whole grain bread and natural peanut butter. Mid-day, she'd make egg-white omelets with spinach and sprouts.

Nico toasted the bread while she cut up fruit, making pretty parfaits that were probably a waste of effort on these two, but she liked it served up this way. Pretty always tasted better.

"Are you excited about Christmas?" She was just making conversation, but she regretted bringing it up knowing all the drama about the holiday plans. It had just slipped out. Kids and Christmas…they just went together.

"Yes." He bounced with enthusiasm. "Now that school's out, it's almost here."

"Do you think you're on Santa's nice list?"

"Definitely. I have some friends in school that might not be, but I know I am."

"Me, too," she said. "I love Christmas. It's my favorite time of the whole year."

"Uncle Drew needs some Christmas decorations. It doesn't even look like Christmas here. You should see my house."

"Is it decorated pretty?"

"Oh, yeah. My stepmom put wreaths on the front doors, and we have a big Christmas tree that looks real. She sprayed stuff on it so it smells real too. I helped put the decorations on it."

"I bet your tree is beautiful. Does it have white lights or colored lights?"

"A *ton* of white lights. You practically need sunglasses, it's so bright. It's super cool."

"It sounds like it! That must have taken a very long time to put them on."

"No. It comes out of the box that way. We just

had to put the ornaments on it. That was easy and fun, too. Before my dad married my stepmom, we only had the tree at the resort. Now we have one at the house, too. I really like that."

"Where I'm from, we go and cut down our own tree," she said.

Nico's eyes lit up. "No way. Does it snow there?"

"It does. Sometimes it snows so much, it's hard to get to the good Christmas trees, and then we have to use the snowmobile to help drag the tree out of the woods."

"That sounds so cool." Nico leaned in, eager to hear more. "I've never seen snow in my whole life. Well, only on TV."

She loved how the idea of snow excited him, but he didn't make a single comment about the cancelled plans. It seemed to her that Drew was more upset about having to cancel the plans than Nico. It was a dream for Nico, but he had no idea what he was missing out on.

Childhood memories flooded back.

"Snow is pretty when it's coming down and finally covers all the grass. It's like a blanket over everything, and it seems quieter. I love snow days. I'd get butterflies in my stomach, and smile so big it made my cheeks hurt." For a moment she was that little girl again. "My sister and I would play outside all day long. Those were such wonderful times."

Nico wore a huge grin. "You look happy just talking about it."

"I am. Thanks for reminding me. Everyone deserves that snow day feeling." She booped him on the nose. "What are you asking Santa for this year?"

"I asked for skis, but then Uncle Drew got hurt…" He shrugged. "I'm glad he didn't get hurt worse though."

That sounded like something his mom had probably said to him.

His excitement returned as quickly as it had faded. "Now I'm asking for a new remote- control dune buggy. They have awesome ones that are really fast. Like 50 mph! Way faster than the one I have, and it can do big jumps. I hope Santa brings that. New tennis shoes, too. The high-top ones like my Uncle Drew wears, and a bow and arrow."

"That sounds like a really good list. Don't need snow for that."

Nico's head cocked slightly to the side. "Snow would've been pretty cool though. I hope I get to play in it someday." His smile had faded, but then he burst into a smile. "Tell me what you like best about the snow?"

She dropped another layer of fruit in each of the parfait cups. "Gosh, I guess making a snowman. Building it is fun, and then decorating him so he seems real. My sister and I would spend all day on one. That's always fun, and snow angels."

"What's a snow angel?"

"You go out in the snow where no one has walked yet, and you lay down in it."

"Isn't it cold?"

"Yeah. Kind of, but you have your coat on, so it's not so bad. You put your hands and feet out like this and then flap your wings and legs." She did a couple of jumping jacks to demonstrate. "When you get up, it looks like an angel was there."

"We do that in the sand on the beach."

"I bet you do. I never even thought of that."

"I can show you one day." He nodded. "I *really* want to see a snowflake."

"Just one?" That tickled her, but she held the giggle inside.

"At least one before I turn nine."

She remembered her childhood with Corinne. They'd loved playing outside in the snow. "When I was your age, we'd play in the bitter cold so long that when we came inside, the heat would feel like it was burning our cheeks. It took forever for us to thaw out." Their mom had to threaten restriction to get them in the house. "My sister and I would put our wet coats and gloves over the heating vent in the kitchen. They were so warm and toasty the next time we went outside."

"That sounds fun."

"It was, but I bet it's fun here, too. It's so awesome that you can play in the water all year long. Even at Christmas."

"We have the tallest Christmas tree on the island at my dad's work."

"Wow! That's lucky. Do you help decorate that, too?"

"No. It's not real. It's made of lights on wires, but in the dark, it looks really cool. There's a star on top that shoots a laser straight up into the sky so Santa doesn't miss his stop here. We're a little island. He could accidentally fly right over if Dad didn't set that up."

He looked as serious as a traffic controller.

"I hadn't even thought of that," she said. "Your dad is really smart."

"*Very* smart." Nico said.

Drew walked into the room. "You must be talking about me."

Nico busted out laughing. "Not this time, Uncle Drew."

"What? You don't think I'm smart?" Drew picked up the boy and swung him in the air and over his head.

"I do, but—" Nico sang out in a fit of giggles.

And then a raucous game of tag ensued, and she hadn't quite heard such a happy noise in all of her life. There'd been a time when she dreamed of having a family. Of afternoon's outside playing with her husband and children, something she'd always wished her parents had done with her and Corinne. They'd always been too busy working.

At that moment, it hit her. She'd always vowed she wouldn't be like her own parents, too busy to enjoy time with family. Yet, here she was. Nowhere close to having a family of her own, and she hadn't made it home for Christmas in a couple of years. *Look what putting work first has gotten me. Here I am, spending the holiday alone with no job, no apartment and no prospects.*

She closed her eyes. *If I ever get so lucky as to meet the right guy and have a family, I'll never let work get in the way of spending time with them.*

CHAPTER TEN

Avery was anxious to talk to Drew about their situation. He didn't realize she'd recognized him, and she was positive he had no idea who she worked for--or used to--or that definitely would've come up in conversation.

She wanted to straighten all of that out, but she also knew that the immediate lift in Drew's spirit was due to that little eight-year-old who'd just started Christmas break. Attitude had a direct correlation to healing just as much as the exercises, rehab, nutrition, and sleep it would take to get this man back in shape.

She refused to shoot holes in Drew Laskin's sails, which seemed to have finally caught wind.

So, she and the guys spent the day playing in the pool, while she snuck in activities that worked all the muscles she needed Drew to work. It went well. Very well. In fact, she rather liked the idea of integrating this into her portfolio for future use if the outcome concluded as she expected. In all the time she'd worked with athletes, pulling them away from their family, the thought had never occurred to her that it could become a family effort, and maybe more enjoyable in the process.

For two days straight, Nico and Drew were inseparable. They set up a tent city in the living room, draping sheets and blankets over tables and chairs to make the biggest fort she'd ever seen.

Nico had insisted on leading her through the maze himself, so she would know where to deliver their hot dogs for dinner, which she'd happily done although Drew's were made of turkey.

When the two of them had finally called it a night, Avery had retired to her room, but she couldn't sleep. So, she put on her robe then quietly went back outside.

The heated pool was a plus. She sat down on the edge and dangled her legs in the water. The cooler nights were pleasant—almost like no weather at all. She stared off into the night sky. The stars seemed so close. If it weren't for the moon, it might be pitch black with no streetlights or homes nearby.

"He's totally smitten with you," Drew said from behind her.

"Hey! You startled me." Her hand covered her heart. "I didn't hear you come out."

"Sorry about that."

"You're talking about Nico? I have a feeling that little boy loves everyone."

"He's a great kid." Drew sat next to her.

"You're really good with him," she said.

"You sound surprised."

"It's a softer side of you that I didn't expect."

"You had me pegged as a stereotypical

egocentric, no-time-for-anyone-but-me kind of guy?"

She winced. He was absolutely right. "I'm sorry. I guess it's an occupational hazard. I run into that a lot. I can see that's not the case with you."

"Thank you," he said. "Nico is easy to be around. Truth is, before my sister got married, I probably was that guy."

"So she lives here on the island."

"Yeah. Brooke's husband was born and raised here. He owns the resort. It's the family business. That's why I bought a place here."

"Where's the rest of your family?"

"We grew up in North Carolina, but it's just me and my sister now. Mom died when we were in high school, and my dad passed away about three years ago."

She couldn't imagine losing both parents so young. It made her feel worse for skipping Christmas at home in Vermont. "I'm sorry. That must've been hard."

"Yeah, he was a great father. He was always there for us. Family has always been important to me, but I love it even more since Brooke got married, and I became an instant uncle to Nico." He sat quietly for a moment. "I could see myself with a couple of kids now. Nico amazes me. He makes me want to be better, to set a good example for him."

"I guess it's hard when your training and on the road. Married to the game."

He shrugged and playfully bumped her shoulder. "Nico has good taste in women."

A charmer like his uncle. "Thank you."

"I didn't mean to heist your private time. I heard you up, and I wanted to thank you for being flexible the last couple of days. I mean, I know this isn't exactly what you're getting paid to do. Entertain my nephew and all."

"As long as you're progressing, it's all good. Laughter and love can cure just about anything." She got up. "I'm going to go try to get some sleep."

"Yeah, sorry. I didn't mean to interrupt—"

"You didn't. I'm just enjoying the end of a really good day." She turned and walked inside.

He followed right behind her, dropping to his knees to crawl into the fort.

Avery giggled, stopping to watch.

"Good night, Avery." The sheets rustled as the grown man worked his way back into the fort with his nephew.

That's a hero.

On the third morning since Nico had started coming over, he surprised Avery with breakfast in bed. She knew Drew was behind it by the shape of the scrambled eggs and bacon on her plate.

"Look. We made a lizard for you," Nico proudly announced. "Uncle Drew says you love lizards."

"Isn't he the nicest man in the world?" It had been sarcastic, but Nico had no idea. He nodded his head.

Drew Laskin was probably a bigger hero than Santa in this little boy's eyes.

That morning while Drew swam laps, Nico told her his plan to ask Santa to send snowflakes for Christmas so everyone could have those snowy-day smiles she'd told him about. His tiny heart touched hers in a way she'd never felt before.

How sweet is it to see the world through those innocent eyes?

She hoped that someday, she could have a little boy of her own who was just as precious as this one.

The days swept by. Avery measured Drew's progress, and even though she hadn't strictly adhered to the rehabilitation plan, the results exceeded their aggressive goals.

Avery put away her goniometer and measuring tape. "You're doing great."

"I have to tell you, this might be in my head, but I feel a hundred percent better than I did just a few days ago," Drew said.

"That's great. You've been working hard. Thanks for following the plan."

"I don't make promises I can't keep."

She believed him. "I appreciate that." She hated that she'd waited this long to tell Drew about the situation, but all this promise talk made her feel guilty. "Drew, we need to talk."

A look of confusion shadowed his expression. "What's wrong?"

"I know who you are," she said.

His head snapped back. "How long have you known?"

"All week."

"Okay." His jaw pulsed. "That long?" He folded his arms across his chest. "You haven't told anyone, have you?"

"No." She shook her head. "Of course not. I'm a professional. I'd never, but there *could be* a problem."

"You're making me nervous. What's the problem?"

She slipped one of her old business cards out of her pants pocket and handed it to him.

He read it, looked at her, then back at the card again. "You're with The Ware Agency?"

"Not anymore, but up until a few days before I came here... Yes, I was."

"I don't understand." His mouth drooped. "Were you spying on me?" The words dripped with disappointment.

"No. Nothing like that." She rubbed her hands together. "I had no idea who you were when I got here. I only took this job to help my sister out of a jam."

"So, let me get this straight. You took time off from your job at the number one sports agency in the nation to help your sister? That doesn't even make sense. Who leaves their perfect little world for something like that?"

"My perfect little world? I'll have you know it was anything but perfect. My position was eliminated. With no notice, Ware pushed me out. You know why?"

"Because you're bossy?"

"No." His comment took her off guard but lightened the mood. "That's what makes me great at what I do, thank you very much."

"Because you were moonlighting when you should've been working?" he guessed.

"No. Because when I first started working there, I accompanied the owner of the company to a few major sporting events. There was nothing between us, but he just got engaged to someone at work, and she would prefer it if I'm no longer around."

"Ouch."

"Yes. So, he eliminated my position to keep the peace," she said. "And did I mention that I lost my corporate apartment too?"

"Three weeks before Christmas? That's not cool at all."

"No, it's not, and so here I am, doing a favor for my sister to buy some time until after the holidays when I can concentrate on finding a job and a place to live."

"I get it. You've been treated unfairly, but at the risk of sounding like a jerk, exactly how is that a problem for me?"

"Because The Ware Agency has been pursuing you."

"That's nothing new. They've been trying to talk me over to that group for a long time." He lifted his eyes to the ceiling. "Wait, I'm putting the pieces together. You're the one that started their wellness program, aren't you?"

"I am."

"You *are* the best. I've got buddies who sing your praises." He pressed his hand to his chin. "Some players have been pushed to play with concussions and injuries that… well, I'm preaching to the choir. You are changing the industry by making the player's health a priority. It's really nice to meet you."

"As much as I'm glad to hear that you appreciate my work, it's unfortunate that Tom Ware will probably not continue that program the way I designed it."

"That's too bad."

"It's out of my hands now. He can do whatever he wants. I signed a non-compete with him, so I, on the other hand, cannot do whatever I want." She pressed her hands together. "This is where our situation becomes a problem."

"I'm not a client. So, I don't see the problem?"

"You're one of the top five. Your face, about the size of the television, is plastered on the focus wall in the boardroom. Well, not this face." She drew a circle in the air around his head. "The clean-cut version of you without all that luxurious hair... or that sexy scruff... and the big smile you have when you're playing with Nico. Which, by the way, I really like it when you smile."

That great smile made an appearance with knee-weakening effect. "So, you like this look?"

She chewed her lower lip. "It's growing on me."

What an understatement.

He stepped closer and her heart rate kicked up. "You're growing on me, too. You're fun when you're not all uptight. Thanks for bringing my smile back."

"Drew, if Tom finds out I'm here, he'll blow this out of the water. He'll be even more determined to get you under contract. He'll ruin you if he can't have you. I wouldn't want to put your career at risk."

"You said yourself I'm going to be fine," he said moving so close that she had to look up at him. Her breath hitched and hung in the back of her throat.

"I know, but—" She placed her hands on his chest because she couldn't help herself.

"I need to keep this quiet. You need to keep this quiet. Fortunately, we're on an island in the middle of the ocean with guard lizards out front."

"I'm never going to live that down, am I?" She eyed him playfully.

"Probably not. It's kind of fun giving you a hard time about it."

"Seriously, Drew, I think it would be best if I left." She pushed away from him, taking a necessary step back to catch her breath. "I'll leave all the instructions here for you. You're on a good track. You and Nico can finish this on your own."

"You can't leave." He closed the gap, reaching for her hand and squeezing it. "Nico really likes having you around."

"Nico is sweet."

"Yeah." Drew looked away, then settled his gaze on her. "Honestly, I like having you here, too. Let's just keep our eye on the ball."

"Baseball analogy? I like it, but—"

"We'll have a nice Christmas here, and then both of us will make New Year's resolutions and have a happy New Year."

"You think it'll be that simple?"

"Why not? You just keep me on task. I wasn't ever going to sign with The Ware Agency, no matter how high the praises were about you or the negotiations they've been making." He lifted his chin. "Here's the thing. Gabe, my agent, he took a chance on me when I was a rookie. I was still wet behind the ears, and he believed in me. I'm not going anywhere. Ware can keep trying to recruit me, but any man crazy enough to let you go the way he did that right before Christmas, well, that's not someone I want representing me."

"That's nice of you to say."

"It's true. Besides, what are the odds of him ever finding out?" Drew shrugged. "You're stuck with me until New Year's."

"Only because I like to see all my patients to the finish line." Could she get through New Year's without falling for this guy? She had to. Good grief, she knew better than to let this happen. Probably a combination of the warm sun and island air impairing her better judgment. "I'm breaking my own rules, which is a first for me, by the way."

"Rules are meant to be broken."

"So I hear." She nodded. *I'm falling for him.* She knew better than to let this happen. Why was he so hard to resist?

Drew must have sensed her sudden apprehension because he rattled on. "We'll do a little shopping tomorrow, and you know what, I think it's time we decorated this place and gave it a holly jolly look. We can make that part of the workout, can't we?"

"We can do extra laps in the store to get our steps in, and while we're decorating, you get to do all the ladder climbing and stretching to the high places. Sound fair?"

"I've got a ton of decorations and stuff out in the garage. Think you can brave the lizards to help me with it?"

"I'm not making any promises I can't keep," she echoed his words. They were more alike than she'd realized.

"I like that in a girl." He walked away, and this time, if she hadn't known he'd been injured, she wouldn't have been able to tell. *Miracles do happen.* Now the real miracle would be if she got through this assignment without a broken heart. *Dear Santa, I think I'm going to need a big dose of Christmas magic to get through this.*

.

CHAPTER ELEVEN

With just three days left before Christmas, Drew's sister finally got back in town. It was great timing, because Drew and Avery hadn't figured out how they were going to surprise Nico with him constantly underfoot.

Drew called Brooke to beg for help. "Hey, Sis. I have you on speakerphone. We need your help. I'm running out of excuses to keep Nico out of the house so we can surprise him by decorating my place for Christmas."

"We?"

"Avery and I." He waited for her to give him a hard time, but she didn't. It wasn't like her to miss an opportunity. "She's going to help me surprise Nico. That kid is crazy about her."

"Sounds like you might be, too."

"Well, I overheard her talking about snow days with him. I think she's going to love this surprise as much as he does, but I need you to keep him away from my place."

"No problem. I've missed that little guy like

crazy. I want to keep him close," Brooke said. "We have baking to do and presents to wrap, and there's a ton of stuff going on at the resort this week. You should bring Avery over with you to the resort when you have some free time."

"We'll try to do that," Drew said, but he knew everything he and Avery were working on was going to take all their time. The plan had gotten bigger and bigger, but what was the fun if not going completely over the top?

"I can't believe you're finally decorating for the holidays," Brooke said. "You've never done that before."

"I know. Why is that?"

"I don't know. I guess I got all the decorating DNA. You just show up for the good time."

"Well, that doesn't sound very nice."

"I'm just teasing. You can't help it if you're the fun twin. This is going to be a great Christmas."

Avery walked into the room. "Hi, Brooke," Avery called out from the doorway.

"Thank you, Avery! Your sister was right. You can do anything. I thought Drew was a lost cause this time the way he was moping around, but you've been like a Christmas angel to our family."

"Thanks for believing in me, Sis," Drew said sarcastically. "You'd be bummed too if you'd just ruined everyone's Christmas plans."

"It wasn't your fault, and not nearly as big a deal as you've been making it. We'll have a wonderful time right here. We can ski another time," Brooke said, and then promised to keep Nico away until Christmas morning.

"Thanks, Sis. We've got to get to work." Drew punched the button to end the call.

He turned to Avery. "We only have a few days to get this done, but I think with the two of us working together we can do it." He raised his hand for a high-five.

Avery slapped it then linked her fingers up with his. "Here we go. Mission: Merry Christmas."

"We've got this."

Drew led the way to the garage. Still sealed, the boxes were stacked five high. Ornaments, lights, wreaths. The works.

"You bought all this stuff and never put them up?" She grabbed six boxes of lights.

"Actually, I did a commercial for this company the year we won the World Series. They sent all this to me for free. There's a huge box with a tree in here somewhere, too. It's supposed to be lifelike. I guess we're about to find out."

By the time they had dragged everything from the garage into the house, it became apparent they didn't need any more decorations. Avery hung the wreaths, and they instantly gave the place a pick-me-up.

"The tree is pre-lit," Avery said as she read the side of the box. "Should we use the rest of these lights inside or outside?"

"I'm out of my league here. What do you think?"

She considering how excited Nico had been about snow. "I have an idea. It might be a little crazy, so you can say no. I promise you won't hurt my feelings if you don't want to do it."

"How crazy can it be?"

"Well, Nico is missing his first white Christmas because you can't travel, right?"

"Thanks for reminding me."

"No. I didn't mean it like that, but does he really have to miss out on snow?"

"I know I'm walking pretty good, but I think at this point, it's best if we stay here."

"I agree. I wasn't suggesting we travel. But why can't we make this place a winter wonderland?"

She could see the ideas chugging in his brain, and then the edges of his mouth turned back up. Lordy, she loved making him smile.

"You're a genius," he said.

"I don't know if we can get our hands on a snow machine, but I know how to make fake snow out of baking soda and hair conditioner," she said. "I've done that before, and it makes pretty fantastic snowballs. They're fluffy and everything."

"There's got to be a video online about how to make a snow machine. I'm pretty handy. I could probably pull that off." He grabbed his phone and started a search.

"We can make snow angels and build a snowman, too," Avery added. "I think it could really be fun."

"And do s'mores over a fire with Christmas carols playing." He turned and pointed at her. "You know we have to have a snowball fight, right?"

"Yeah. Of course. I can make the snowballs. I'll make a hundred for each of you! We can even build cardboard igloo bunkers. That would be so fun. Easy too. You have about a gazillion shipping boxes stacked up in the garage. All we need is some tape. If we wrap them in white paper, or plastic trash bags that might be better, so they don't get soggy."

"And look more realistic." He reached over, placed his hands on the sides of her face, and kissed her square on the mouth. "You are the best."

She stood there, mouth agape.

He didn't let her overthink it. Instead he swept her into his arms and twirled her. "This is going to be an awesome white Christmas."

Emotions reeling, a nervous giggle escaped. Good grief, she'd turned into a breathless, giggling teenager! "I'll draw out a plan."

"As you must," he teased.

She grabbed her notebook and sketched out all of their ideas, then divvied up the work. "It's a ton to get done, but if we divide and conquer, we can do this."

"We make a pretty good team." Drew took the sheet of paper and tore it in half. "First on my list is the Christmas tree. I'll get started on that now."

It didn't take five minutes to unpack and position the tree. It was a good one. It didn't even require a ton of fluffing and tweaking of the limbs to give it a good shape. They shimmied it into place, and Avery spread a shiny red tree skirt around the bottom. With one press of the button on the remote, the entire Christmas tree lit up.

Avery hung ornaments while Drew continued to play with the remote, changing the colors of the lights. Blue. Green. Red. White. Multicolor and running lights that made her a little dizzy.

"I think we should stick to the colored lights. No

blinking." She handed him two shiny bell-shaped ornaments. "Hang these toward the middle. They are too pretty to hide."

He hung them, and with each shiny bauble they added, the tree looked even more festive.

She opened a box printed with a knit sweater design on the front. "Oh gosh, look at these crossed wooden ski decorations. Are they cute, or what?" The wooden skis were hand-painted with snowflakes and even had miniature metal bindings and ski poles.

"Yeah. I like the see-through balls the best, though. They look cool in front of the lights."

"They really do glisten. It makes me feel..." She took in a deep breath, searching for the words. "Joy. That's what I'm feeling."

"Joyful? Yeah, you know that perfectly describes what I'm feeling, too. Actually, I don't think I've ever understood real joy until this minute." He held her gaze for a long moment. "Avery. I'm really glad you're here."

Fear raced through her. "Me, too." She grabbed the tree topper hoping the subject change would calm her. "Time to put the star on top. Do you have a ladder?"

"Sure thing. Wait here."

Avery took a few pictures of the work in progress, then added a couple more items to the shopping list.

Drew came back and steadied the ladder close the tree. "Hand me the tree topper?"

She carried the colorful glass star over to him. His fingertips grazed her arm as he took it from her.

Her heart pounded as she watched him position the star.

"Is it straight?"

Red, green, gold, white, and blue danced across the room from the twenty-six-point star. "It's perfect." *The whole day was.*

Drew stepped down from the ladder and slipped his arm around her waist. "We did good."

A tingle raced through her. "Stockings," she tried to say evenly. She turned and pointed at him. "We need stockings."

"Get one for you and me, too," Drew said.

She started to add them to her list, then pursed her lips like a puffer. "You think *you're* on the nice list, Mister?" She swept her ink pen in the air like an X.

"What? You don't think I'm nice?"

"Cranky, but nice." She twisted the list in her hand. "I'm going to go to town and pick up this stuff. You need to stretch and do your exercises. We'll finish up when I get back. Deal?"

"Yes, if you're sure you don't need my help."

"No. I can get it. You get moving." She jogged to her bedroom to get her purse.

The doorbell rang just as she closed the door behind her. She couldn't wait to meet Brooke in person. She knew Brooke and Drew were twins, but she couldn't imagine a feminine version of Drew.

She hitched her purse on her shoulder and started back down the hall. Drew answered the door with a hearty hello, but what followed made her turn and run back to her room.

CHAPTER TWELVE

"That has got to be the biggest gift basket I've ever seen," Drew said. "You can set it on the table. If it'll fit."

A man ambled into the foyer, hovering near in the hallway table which was clearly not deep enough for the basket.

"The floor, I guess," Drew said. *Is that a showerhead hanging in there?* Through the red cellophane, he could see a blender and a pair of sneakers, too. "Who is this from?"

"From me." The man poked his head around the side of the basket. "I'm Tom Ware of The Ware Agency. Nice to meet you." He set the unexpected gift on the floor and extended his hand.

The bullet-shaped man looked about ready to suffer a heat stroke in that suit. Beads of sweat pooled above his brow.

Drew stood there registering what had just happened. That one in seven hundred thousand had just become one in one. He'd just let the enemy right in. He hoped Avery wouldn't walk right into this mess.

Realization swept through him. "How did you get through the gate?" He pushed his hand in his pocket, squaring off with the guy.

"Merry Christmas, man. I wanted to deliver this personally." His tight grip was practiced, as was the clap on Drew's back. "I'm a huge fan."

"I asked you a question."

"I'm the best negotiator around. A skill that gets me pretty much everything I want, including through your gate, which apparently has a code that the limo driver knows. Although to his credit, he wasn't easy to persuade." His lip twitched. "Everyone has a price." He laughed, then lifted his chin. "You've got a price, don't ya?"

"No. Actually, money has never been a driving factor for me."

"Sure you do, son. Everyone does." The man walked through the foyer as if he were assessing the value of the house. "Your contract's coming up for renegotiation. You know, I've clinched the last few big deals with your ball club. I bet ol' Gabe can't get close to the numbers I've been getting. You gonna invite me in?"

"No. Actually, I'm not. I don't do business over the holidays."

Ware didn't look too pleased. His nostrils flared, but he recovered quickly. "My apologies. I didn't mean to intrude. Let me just lay out a couple things for you, and then I'm on my way. I have some parties in the Hamptons to get to. You're welcome to come along if you like. There'll be big commercial endorsements looking for the right face." He eyed Drew. "You're going to shave that off, aren't you? Not really your best look."

"I just said I don't do business over the holidays. I'm spending time with my family." Drew took a step toward the front door, trying to force Tom back that way.

"We're the best agency. Number one, and you deserve the best."

"Thank you," but the words came out tight, and he didn't care if it sounded polite or not at this point.

"I also happen to have the top sports medicine team at your complete disposal."

"Really?" Drew wished his brow hadn't arched like that, but the nerve of this guy. "I'm healthy but tell me more."

"You haven't heard?"

I heard you let Avery go right here before the holidays.

Tom rambled on about the exclusive sports wellness program his agency offered. "A customized plan for every single one of our athletes. This isn't a one-size-fits-all physical therapy team. This is sports medicine at its finest. We're protecting you. Doing everything possible to maximize your career and earning potential. How's that sound?"

"Impressive. Who designed that?"

"Proprietary," he said taking credit. "All in-house. The very best."

Drew's stomach turned. "You know, now that I think about it, I did hear about what you're doing over there. Didn't Avery Troupe set that program up for you?" He clicked his fingers. "Yeah, I'd love to talk to her."

Tom looked like he'd swallowed a rotten egg. "Her entire team is excellent. No shortcuts, either."

"You get me a meeting with Avery Troupe after the first of the year, then maybe we can talk."

Drew saw the fleeting nanosecond of panic, but the guy recovered quickly. A skilled liar.

"You're on," Tom said. "I can absolutely make that happen. I'll be in touch." Tom made haste for the door. Probably afraid he'd promise something else he couldn't deliver.

Drew stood there, watching as Tom got back into the one black limousine on the island. Drew dialed his phone as the car pulled away. "Jax. It's Drew. Don't say a word. You've got Tom Ware in your limo. I know he paid you off to get down my driveway. Be sure he goes straight to the airport and gets on a plane off this island, or you won't be driving me anymore. Call me when he leaves. Got it?"

"Yes, sir. I'm dropping a customer off, and then I'll call when I'm on the way back to schedule that with you. Merry Christmas." Jax disconnected the call.

When Drew turned around, Avery was standing behind him as pale as the snow-white shirt she wore.

"One more minute, and I'd have run right into him in the driveway." She looked shaken.

"But you didn't."

"You know, I pride myself in being unflappable. You were a challenge in the beginning, and I handled it. But this? This is more than I can take. I can't let my problems interfere with your career."

A smile crept across his face. His defenses lowered, there was nothing he could do about it.

"Then don't worry," he said.

"I promise I didn't let anyone know I was here."

"I believe you."

"What will happen next?" Her phone rang from the kitchen.

Drew laughed. "Three guesses who that is."

She let it go to voicemail. "That's the first time I've ever known him to deliver one of those baskets personally. He is determined to get you on his team. He won't give up easily. You could probably talk him down a few percentages on his fee."

"No way. I'm committed to Gabe. And besides, I'm making more than enough money as it is."

"Just as well. Tom has no filter, no tact, no idea about boundaries. No loyalty either. All he wants is the next big deal."

"Come on. Sit with me. His driver will call to let me know when he's off the island. Until then, let's just hang out by the pool and get back in Christmas mode. We can talk through what's left to do on that plan you wrote up. I know how you love plans." He took her hand, singing Jingle Bells as he led her outside.

Drew quit singing when they got outside. "I have to admit, it felt pretty good to kick that guy out of my house." They sat in the loungers under the pergola. "He's going to beg you to come back, Avery, and then you can give have the satisfaction of telling him no."

"I won't lie. That will feel good. It won't fix not having a job, but it'll be a start."

Not even thirty minutes later, Jax called Drew to let him know that Tom Ware's helicopter had just taken off from the airport.

"He's gone." Drew tucked his phone in his pocket. "Time to shop. I'll drive. Your mission, should you choose to accept it, is it to get everything on that list in less than two hours, so we can get back and spend the rest of the night making Christmas magic."

He hummed a few bars of the *Mission Impossible* theme song, then waited for an answer.

She hummed along with him. "I've got the list. Let's do this before we self-destruct." They ran out the door and hopped in the golf cart. "We're going to make even Santa Claus proud."

CHAPTER THIRTEEN

Late on Christmas Eve, they finally had completed every single task in their extravagant plan. Drew shut off the living room lights and turned on the tree.

"It looks fantastic," Avery said. "Better than I'd ever dreamed."

Borax and pipe cleaner snowflakes she'd spent all day making now hung from the ceiling on fishing line at all different heights. Each one varied in size and shape, just like the real thing.

"Nico is going to go wild. Heck, my sister is going to go wild, too. She loves snow. By the way, during the snowball fight, her arm is as good as mine, so watch out."

"Good to know." Her face squinched. "I throw like a girl."

He reached over and tickled her. "Maybe you should be on my team, anyway."

"Works for me," she said wriggling away with a squeal.

"You are really ticklish!"

"You discovered my one weakness," she teased.

Drew got up and walked over to the stack of presents next to the Christmas tree. "Look at this."

"What? Did one of the bows fall off?" She got to her feet to get one from the hall closet where they'd tucked away all the wrapping supplies.

"No. Come here." He sat in the floor.

She ran through her mental checklist wondering what could be amiss. Confused, she walked over to him.

"This is for you." He handed her the box. "From me."

She paused, lowering herself next to him. "You bought me a gift?"

He reached under the tree again. "And this one. I bought you two."

"Drew. I didn't get you anything. Why did you—"

He cocked his head playfully. "Just open them."

She opened the red package first, tearing through the paper like a ten-year-old. She lifted the top of the box and pushed back the tissue paper. "Flannel?" She held the garment up in front of her. "Onesie pajamas?"

He nodded. "Yeah. I'm getting ready to crank the air conditioning down as low as it will go, so when Nico gets here in the morning and sees all these snowflakes you made along with the snowballs, I want it to feel like snow weather in here, too. That's half the fun, right?"

"That's a great idea." She lifted the garment from the box. "Oh wow. They have feet!"

"They seemed appropriate for a family

89

Christmas morning."

Family. "They're perfect." She fanned her face trying to resist the tears that threatened to fall.

"Are you crying?"

"No. Maybe. Just happy, fun tears. This was really sweet." She hugged them to her chest. "I love them so much."

"You might be tough on the outside, but there is a soft, gooey center inside you, isn't there? And not just for lizards."

"Real funny." He did bring out something soft inside her. Something she'd never felt before.

"If I'd had time, I'd have had a lizard embroidered on them."

"Why doesn't that surprise me?"

"Because you're getting to know me," he said. "Really know me, like no one else. You are the best thing my sister has ever done for me."

"A happy accident in a seemingly disastrous chain of events," she said, trying to dismiss the comment, but she knew what he meant. "I feel the same way. I should be a wreck. No job. No home. No idea where to begin to repair my situation, and yet I'm enjoying the moment. It's because of you."

"You can open the other present in the morning. It's a ski jacket. It matches mine. And Nico's, and my sister's, and brother-in-law's. There's one for each of us. From Santa. We'll all be wearing puffy jackets with fur trim."

"We'll look festive."

"We sure will. Morning is going to come early. We better call it a night."

She stood, clutching her pajamas. "Good. I can't

wait to put these on."

He reached out and squeezed her hand. "I'll see you in the morning?"

"Count on it."

"Oh, I am." There was no teasing in that comment.

She was tired of following her own rules, so she reached up and kissed him gently on the lips. "Thank you, Drew." Athlete or not, her heart was making up its own rules with every breath she took, and she was taking a liking to both—the rules and the guy.

When Avery's alarm went off at six o'clock Christmas morning, her nose was so cold it stung. It really did feel like a cold, damp, winter morning. She put her feet on the floor, thankful for the footies.

"Ho, ho, ho," followed the knock at her bedroom door.

She opened the door and struck a pose, modeling the fun pajamas he'd gifted her. "Best gift ever." She realized his pajamas matched hers. He should have looked ridiculous, but to her, he looked amazing because he wanted to create a perfect Christmas for his nephew. What woman could resist that? "Oh my gosh. You didn't tell me we were going to be twins. This is great."

"Once a twin, always a twin," he teased. "You look better in yours." He gave her a quick up and down. "Never in all my life would I have thought red plaid flannel pajamas could be sexy, but..." He reached for her hand and twirled her. "You look like a present."

"I am." She looked into his eyes. "Yours. Merry Christmas?"

"The best Christmas present ever." He pulled her into his arms. "I cannot wait to unwrap you."

She snuggled against him.

"I hate the timing of this, but my sister just called. They're on the way over." He groaned, then dropped a kiss on her neck.

"We'd better hurry, then. Come on!" Holding hands, they raced into the living room. With the air conditioning blowing on high, and the ceiling fans spinning, the snowflakes moved from the fishing line like the real thing.

"It looks so good! I hope your air conditioning system doesn't totally freeze up. I didn't know you could get a house this cold."

"Surprised me, too," Drew said.

A golf cart pulled into the driveway.

Drew started the Christmas music from his phone, and it blasted out of the speakers around the room.

At that precise moment, Nico came through the front door wearing a suit made out of red ski-sweater pattern material with snowmen on it, and those well-known first big-band chords of "It's the Most Wonderful Time of the Year" filled the house.

Avery took pictures. Even through the small

screen on her phone, she could see the excitement in Nico's face, and Brooke's too.

"What have y'all done!" Brooke's eyes were as wide as Nico's. "It's gorgeous."

"It's winter in here," Nico yelled. "Look at all the snowflakes, Dad!"

Avery loved how Brooke and her husband wore matching Christmas shirts, and Nico's suit was the same exact red. They were Christmas card perfect. She snapped another picture.

Drew whispered to Avery. "Cover me until I get the snowblower going, then bring them out there."

"I'm on it." She let Nico, Brooke, and Nate check out the Christmas tree and admire all the gifts until she heard the snow machine engage. "Isn't it crazy? We woke up and everything was like this." With the music so loud, they hadn't heard it start up outside. Avery corralled them toward the patio doors.

"Come here," she said. "You have to see this." Avery rushed them along. When she opened the back door, she stepped out of the way so they could see all snowflakes falling over the backyard and pool.

"Wow!" Nico raced outside in a fit of giggles. He threw his arms in the air, trying to catch the snow. "How?"

Avery's heart soared. This was the best Christmas gift ever.

"It's snowing. It's real snow! Look!" Nico jumped up and down.

Igloo bunkers had been setup on each side of the patio. Penguin sentries wearing Drew's baseball jersey's, one in home colors, the other in away, stood in front of each bunker.

Drew snuck over and inserted himself back in the conversation.

Nico, in all seriousness, said, "I know how this happened."

Drew gave Avery a look. Nico was smart. Of course, he wasn't fooled.

"I asked Santa to bring snowflakes this year so we could all experience snow day smiles. It worked!"

Drew's smile could have led Santa's sleigh through the thickest fog right then, and Avery fell even harder for him. "Well, Nico, if anyone deserves all their dreams to come true, it's you. You had to have been on the tip-top of Santa's list."

"I was pretty good," Nico agreed.

"You must have been. Let's open presents," Drew said.

They went inside and Avery served up a healthy breakfast casserole while they oohed and ahhed over the gifts and tried to figure out how to put the toys together.

"Look, Avery. Santa brought you a present, too," Nico said. "And a stocking!"

Avery took the box that held the jacket in it from Drew. It had really been sweet of him to make her a part of the family for the day. "Oh my gosh. Thank you. I can't believe he found me here."

"Santa knows everything." Nico's sincerity was unmistakable. "I got you something too, Avery."

"You did?"

"Yes, ma'am. I got it in our gift shop. Mom said

I could." He carried a small box wrapped in red and white striped paper with a metallic gold bow on top over to her.

"He insisted," Brooke added.

"This is so thoughtful. Thank you." Nico had clearly wrapped it himself. There was more tape than paper securing it, but she finally got into it.

Avery lifted the delicate gold chain from the box. From it hung a tiny lizard with ruby-jeweled eyes.

"Uncle Drew told me you love lizards," he said proudly.

She flashed Drew a look, who had just about spit out his orange juice from laughing so hard. Finally, he swallowed and wiped his mouth. "It's a long story, Sis. I'll have to tell you that one."

"I can't wait," Brooke said.

Avery hugged Nico. "I love it. I'm going to put it on right now. Thank you so much." She squeezed him. "You are the best."

Drew helped her with the clasp, whispering, "I really wish I'd thought of this."

She wrapped her fingers around the dangling charm. "It's precious. I will always love this lizard."

Once they'd all emptied their stockings, which at some point Drew had filled with fresh fruit and those wacky paddles with the ball on elastic that prompted a competition between them all. Finally, they unwrapped their last Santa gifts, the puffy jackets with the fur trim, and went outside to get the snowball fight going.

Teams took their places, and for the next forty minutes, an all-out snow ball fight took place in Drew's backyard under a warm, island sun.

Somehow, Nico had never even noticed that it had been Drew aiming all the snowflakes over the backyard from behind the pool house wall. He really did believe that Santa had made it snow, and Drew didn't seem to mind not getting the credit one bit which made Avery just appreciate him more.

Avery went inside to her room to call home while Drew and the rest of them helped Nico build his first snowman out of the fluffy un-meltable mixture that she'd put together. She'd made enough to fill three big boxes, so they had snow to spare for any size snowman, or a couple of smaller ones.

She dialed Mom and Dad's number. "Hi, Daddy. It's Avery."

"Merry Christmas, my littlest elf. We're missing you. Let me get your mother."

She waited until they were both on the phone. "Hey, Avery. We were just talking about you. We wish you were here."

"Me too, Mom."

"We got our big holiday basket from the agency yesterday morning," Mom said.

Dad chimed in, "Before seven in the morning. I hadn't even had my coffee yet."

"You did?" Drew was right. Tom was going to pull out all the stops. Avery knew that delivery had to have been a last-minute decision by Tom, because those baskets were always delivered in the middle of December. She hoped Tom had had to deliver it on Christmas Eve himself. Even better if that had made him late for his own wedding.

"It's even bigger than last year," Dad said.

"Oh goodness. Well, I hope there's something in

it you like."

"Your dad is already wearing the Carolina Panthers hat," Mom said.

Avery wanted to blurt out the truth about her job at agency right then, but that would only ruin their day. She held back and let them give her an update.

Afterwards she told them she'd be in town for Corinne's New Year's Eve party. "Are you two coming to that?"

"No," Dad said, "but you can all come over for New Year's Day dinner. Your mother will have all the necessary foods to be sure we have luck, and money, and love, and everything else."

"I'll be there," Avery said.

"Merry Christmas, honey," Dad said. "We can't wait to see you."

Avery hung up the phone feeling a little homesick. Losing her job had felt like the end of the world a few weeks ago. When had her priorities gotten so off track? Family should've been first.

She walked back into the living room to find Drew sitting on the floor next to the Christmas tree by himself.

"Did everyone leave?" she asked.

"Yeah. They have a big thing at the resort. We'll catch up with them tonight. I hope you'll come with me. Dinner, dancing. They even do fireworks."

"Sure. That sounds fun."

"I haven't been this happy in a long time," Drew said.

She sat on the floor next to him. Her thoughts did a news-reel version of the day: all their hard work turning the place into a Winter Wonderland.

97

Mission accomplished. "Me either, and I'm glad you're feeling back to your old self."

"Better than my old self. Because of you."

She could feel the heat climb from her chest and neck. "I like you this way. You're a lot of fun when you're not cranky."

"Was I that cranky?"

"Not for long," she admitted. "I just got off the phone with my folks. Tom delivered one of those crazy baskets to them. I think you're right. He's going to try to deliver me to you on a silver platter."

Drew laced his fingers with hers. "Do I need him to make that happen?"

She looked at him, almost afraid to ask if he was teasing. "He can't deliver me. I wouldn't give him the time of day. There's no amount of money that would persuade me to work for him again, no matter how iron-clad my non-compete is."

"I'm glad to hear that. Think I could talk you into sticking around here for a while?"

"I have plans on New Year's Eve at my sister's house for a party, and then New Year's Day at Mom and Dad's." She hesitated, then went all in. This was someone who'd won her time and attention, and in the process, her heart. She wasn't going to let him slip away. "If you come with me, then I could stay until then, and come back with you after. I don't have a job to get back to."

"I like the sound of that." Drew leaned over and kissed her. "Maybe you could be my personal sports therapist for the season. You know, just to be sure I don't get hurt."

"No." She shook her head emphatically. "I have

a rule about mixing business and pleasure."

"Rules are meant to be broken."

"I've heard that somewhere before." She wagged her finger in his direction. "Was it you that said that?"

"I believe so. See how well it worked for me?" He pulled her close.

She wrapped her arms around his neck. "You do look very happy." Happiness twirled inside her, too. "Fly to Vermont with me for the New Year's Eve party at my sister's."

"Are you tempting me with a good time?"

Avery didn't hesitate. "Kiss me at midnight under the mistletoe and you have a deal."

"We definitely have a deal," he said.

"I can be your personal trainer for the season...very personal." Avery waggled her eyebrows playfully.

He kissed her on the forehead, then her nose, and then her lips, where the kiss became long and slow. "Like that?" he said against her lips.

She moaned in agreement. "Yes. Exactly like that."

"Merry Christmas, Avery. I can't wait to see what the year ahead looks like, but I know it will be a good one with you by my side." He took her phone from her hand. "Oh, just one more thing." He pulled up her contact list and blocked Tom Ware's phone number. "Now, we're sure to have a perfect year."

"I like the way you think." She hugged him, her forehead against his. "Merry Christmas, Drew."

"A very Merry Christmas. I have one last present

to unwrap," he said with a playful growl.

"So this is Christmas magic." Avery settled into his arms. "Merry Christmas to me."

Thank you for reading
MISSION: Merry Christmas

Did you enjoy this sweet holiday story?

**Please STOP to leave a review now,
and then recommend this story to your friends.**

Your review helps lead other readers to my books, and that's the best gift a reader can give to an author.

With gratitude,
Nancy

Enjoy the following snowflake designs you can make for your home, a recipe for crystalized snow flake ornaments, and an excerpt from *Christmas Angels,* first book set in Antler Creek.

Enjoy the following excerpt from
Christmas Angels, **first book set in Antler Creek.**

Download a book checklist with reading order –
FREE on Nancy's website.

Christmas Angels

Nancy Naigle ©2019

Back Cover Copy

Growing up, Liz Westmoreland dreamed of taking over her grandparents' inn located in the small mountain town of Antler Creek only for it to be sold before she ever got the chance. While browsing the internet, she stumbles upon a listing for what looks to be the picturesque inn and it's set to go to auction. Liz places a bid, and by a miracle, wins the auction. But when she gets there, she finds the property in significant disrepair.

When Matt Hardy narrowly lost the inn and property that butted his land, he just hoped it wasn't another city slicker coming to make matters worse after the previous owners gutted the place for an art gallery. But the minute he recognized the sweet, freckle-faced girl from his childhood and heard her plans to reopen the inn, he jumps at the chance to help his childhood crush restore a place where he made so many fond memories.

While working on repairs, Liz and Matt discover her grandmother's collection of angels in one of the cabins. When the angels start mysteriously showing up all over the inn, she begins to look at them as reassurance—that restoring the inn is what she's meant to do. But when an accident leaves Liz feeling like she made a mistake, will Matt—and the residents of Antler Creek—be able to show Liz that she's found a home? And possibly true love as well?

CHRISTMAS ANGELS EXCERPT

CHAPTER ONE

Liz motioned for Dan to follow her to the kitchen island. "Look at this. I'm sure it's my grandparents' old place."

"You haven't been back there in what? Twenty years?" Dan pulled the computer closer and looked at the listing.

"Maybe fifteen-ish."

"Nice. Yeah. Wait. What are you thinking?" Dan lifted his gaze, then cocked his head. "You're not seriously considering—"

"I've been waiting for this my whole life. Angels Rest is practically mine." Excitement forced her words out in a flurry. "So, how do I do this auction thing?"

"You don't." He closed the top of the computer, and handed her a barbecue sandwich. "Not without going to see the condition of the house and checking to make sure you're not also buying old liens against the place."

"There's no time. It goes up for auction in the morning. I've read through the FAQ's, it doesn't look that complicated. I need to get a proof of funds letter from my banker before I can bid though."

"You're going to bid on this place sight unseen? I have to advise against it, Liz. That's just plain crazy." Dan ran a hand through his hair. "You're always talking about situations being a 'sign'; well, maybe this is a sign that you should let this crazy idea go once and for all."

"No. It's not a sign to let it go. Finding out the day before Angels Rest goes up for auction is a sign it's meant to be." She scooted closer to him and opened the laptop again. "Look at these. The pictures don't look so bad. Okay, so it's overgrown, but that's cosmetic."

"Pictures can hide a multitude of problems. Very expensive ones, and the fact that there are only three pictures total is a red flag, especially since only one shows the house. The other is an aerial. You have no idea what it looks like inside."

"It's rustic. It's a timber home, what could go wrong?"

"Termites?"

He had a point. "Well, the thing is still standing."

"You have no way of really knowing that without going and taking a professional with you to check it out." Dan leaned against the counter. "Why are you so hell-bent on this idea? You're good at what you do. You have a good life here. Why the heck would you want to move to the mountains?"

"I loved spending time with my grandparents. The mountains are like an old friend to me. The nature. The quiet. I always thought I'd rent rooms out to people, and help them enjoy the area just like Gram and Pop. It was a good and pleasing way of life."

"You'd be bored out of your skull up there. No shopping. Probably no pizza delivery. You do love pizza."

"I can make my own pizza."

He cocked his head.

"I could learn."

"You love your job."

"I wouldn't say I love it. I'm good at it. But I could still do some projects if I get bored. I love that place. It's why I've worked so hard and saved for so long. Every bonus, every raise—I've invested it all for this one dream."

Dan folded his arms. "So that's why I couldn't get you to look at a new house last year?"

"Exactly. I told you. I have everything I need here. I've got money socked away for a new place." She raised her eyebrows.

"The right place. The one that I've had in my heart since as long as I can remember."

"But a person in your position should live in a much nicer house in a much better area of the city. Maybe you'd be happier here if—"

"There's nothing wrong with this house or my neighborhood. Or Angels Rest."

"I didn't say there was. Your house will be an easy sell, but I just didn't think you were really serious about a house in the mountains."

"You never listen to what I say." Which was fine, really. It would be a different story if he were her boyfriend, but their relationship wasn't like that.

"I do listen. Kind of. I guess I just didn't put two and two together."

"Well, call it four and help me, why don't you?" He handed her a plate with barbecue, slaw, baked beans, and corn bread on it. "Do you know how much work a place like that could take?"

"I can take a leave of absence to do the renovation. It won't be much different from what I do on a daily basis, but instead of opening a mega-retail site I'll be opening an inn. I can do contract work from up there and do both for a while until I build up a clientele."

"You really have thought this through."

"I've been dreaming of it for years, Dan." She walked into the living room with her plate and plopped down on the sofa.

"You just don't get it. My grandparents owned this inn on the mountainside of Antler Creek. What are the odds of me finding this out the night before it goes on sale?"

He sat down in one of the chairs and balanced his plate on his knee. "One in a million, I'm sure."

"Right. Each summer," Liz said, "people came not just to Antler Creek, but to my grandparents' inn for the fishing and fireside cookouts, and every winter they came for the skiing and Christmas festivities. The inn was known for the best Christmas lights around. You could see them from down in the valley. People came from miles around." In her mind she was back there, bundled up and excited as people began to join together. "There were carriage rides up the mountain to see the lights up close. Gram would make hot chocolate and her secret-recipe cookies for visitors. I helped. It was magical."

Dan took out his phone and started typing. "And today the population in Antler Creek is eleven hundred twenty-nine, and twenty-five years ago the population was twelve hundred thirty-four."

So there wasn't much growth. That was just year-round population. "A steady population," she reasoned.

"A stagnant one."

"It's not about the population. Or maybe it is. Antler Cree is quaint. It's the perfect place to relax. I loved spending time there."

"That was a long time ago, Liz. And you haven't been back in years. What's that say about it?"

She shut her mouth. That was a fair point. "It broke my heart a little that my grandparents left it behind. I'd always assumed I'd take it over from them."

"What will your guests do with their time when they stay with you?"

"All the things they used to. Enjoy nature. Fly-fishing. Antiquing. Hike to the waterfall. Pop led hikes and fishing excursions nearly every week." Am I really brave enough to do this?

"I guess the waterfall would still be there," he said. "Are you going to take strangers on hikes in the woods? That sounds like a recipe for disaster."

"Why not? And fly-fishing on the stream was amazing in the summer. I used to be quite good at it."

He sighed. "You know I'm not going to wade out in cold water and fish, right?"

She shrugged. This wasn't about the two of them. He knew that too. "You can visit. I promise to have Wi-Fi."

His mouth tugged to the side the way it did

when he was disappointed.

"Be happy for me," she said. "Please?"

He sucked in a deep breath. "I'm still not saying this is a good idea, but if you're going to do it be careful. The sale is as-is, where-is, so if you win, you're stuck with it even if it's a hunk of termite-ridden rubbish."

"I hear you. You've made your point, but I'm also stuck with it if it's exactly like I remember, and that would be awesome." She grinned so wide her lashes tickled her cheeks.

"I head to Denver tomorrow night for my cousin's wedding,"

Dan said. "Are you sure I can't talk you into coming with me instead? It'll be a great party and a fun long weekend. Could save you six figures."

She'd declined the invitation weeks ago. "No thanks. I've got things to do around here that I've neglected the past couple of months while I was working in South Carolina." She took in a long deep breath, crossed her fingers, and held them up. "Or I might own a new home." He rolled his eyes, and shoved the last bit of barbecue into his mouth. "I'll be back Tuesday. Keep me posted."

The next morning, Liz had met with her banker, submitted her proof of funds, and finished her entries on the auction portal with little time to spare before the auction began.

Like Dan, her banker had given her a speech about buying a property at auction sight unseen. He hadn't seemed any less concerned when she mentioned that she used to spend every summer and winter there as a kid, and that she had a good feeling about this. It might have sounded like an impulse purchase to him, but she'd been wishing, hoping, and planning for this for years. It was surely meant to be. It didn't really matter what his personal thoughts were. This was her decision, and her money, and she had the proof of funds letter in hand. She was set.

Purchase Christmas Angels to continue reading.

ANTLER CREEK NOVELS
Christmas Angels
What Remains True
…more to come.

Make your own paper snowflakes.

Cut out this page to make your
snowflake, then trace more!

How to create your own snowflake masterpieces.

Lucky for us, no two snowflakes are alike, so there are no #fails when it comes to making these.

You'll just need paper and scissors. Cut your paper into a square. If you're using regular 8.5 x 11 paper, just trim the bottom half off to get an 8.5 x 8.5" square. Any size square will do!

Fold like this…and then snip away!

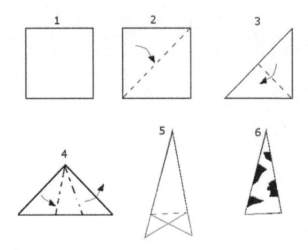

Add salt crystals to your snowflakes for a super snowy look.

1. Spoon 3 tablespoons of salt into a bowl.
2. Add just enough hot water to dissolve the salt, and stir.

3. Place your snowflakes on a sheet pan, and pour salt water solution on top making sure the entire snowflake is covered.

4. Set aside for a few days until the water has evaporated and the salt has crystallized giving your snowflake texture.

Hang and enjoy.

ABOUT THE AUTHOR

***USA TODAY* and ECPA Bestselling Author
Nancy Naigle** whips up small-town love stories
with a dash of suspense and a whole lot of heart.
Now happily retired, she devotes her time to
writing, antiquing, crafting and the occasional spa
day with friends. Nancy has published over thirty
titles, with several movies appearing on the
Hallmark Channel, and her ECPA bestselling novel,
The Shell Collector can be found streaming on FOX
Nation. A native of Virginia Beach, she currently
calls the Blue Ridge Mountains home.

More on Nancy and her books, movies, social
media and newsletter links can be found at
www.NancyNaigle.com.

Made in the USA
Monee, IL
14 November 2022

17704877R00075